DANCE DIVAS

Let's Rock!

DANCE DIVAS

Showtime!

Two to Tango

Let's Rock!

Step It Up
(coming soon)

DANCE DIVAS

Let's Rock!

Sheryl Berk

BLOOMSBURY
NEW YORK   LONDON   NEW DELHI   SYDNEY

First published in the United States of America in June 2014
by Bloomsbury Children's Books
www.bloomsbury.com

Bloomsbury is a registered trademark of Bloomsbury Publishing Plc

For information about permission to reproduce selections from this book, write to
Permissions, Bloomsbury Children's Books, 1385 Broadway, New York, New York 10018
Bloomsbury books may be purchased for business or promotional use. For information on
bulk purchases please contact Macmillan Corporate and Premium Sales Department at
specialmarkets@macmillan.com

Library of Congress Cataloging-in-Publication Data
Berk, Sheryl.
Let's rock! / Sheryl Berk.
pages   cm.   — (Dance Divas ; #3)
Summary: When the girls in the Dance Divas dance team fight over the lead in a
new music video, Miss Toni decides to teach the girls a lesson about teamwork.
ISBN 978-1-61963-225-7 (paperback) • ISBN 978-1-61963-224-0 (hardcover)
ISBN 978-1-61963-226-4 (e-book)
[1. Dance teams—Fiction. 2. Dance—Fiction.] I. Title.
PZ7.B45236Le 2014   [Fic]—dc23   2013050273

Book design by Donna Mark
Typeset by Westchester Book Composition
Printed and bound in the U.S.A. by Thomson-Shore Inc., Dexter, Michigan
2 4 6 8 10 9 7 5 3 1 (paperback)
2 4 6 8 10 9 7 5 3 1 (hardcover)

All papers used by Bloomsbury Publishing, Inc., are natural, recyclable products
made from wood grown in well-managed forests. The manufacturing processes
conform to the environmental regulations of the country of origin.

*To Debbie Kahn, my little sis, and
the fifth Beatle*

Table of Contents

DANCE DIVAS
* Let's Rock!

CHAPTER 1

All Smiles

Liberty Montgomery skipped through the doors of Dance Divas Studio Monday evening and headed straight for the dressing room.

"Hi, all!" She smiled at her teammates. "Everyone having a nice day?"

Scarlett Borden, the Divas' unofficial dance-team captain, stared at her. "You okay, Liberty?" she asked, genuinely concerned. "You didn't fall and bump your head or something, did you?"

"No, silly! Why?" Liberty answered, beaming from ear to ear.

"Because you put the *diva* in Dance Divas,"

Rochelle Hayes said. Rock knew Liberty would never just bounce into a rehearsal all smiles without a reason. And that reason usually involved her getting a solo, a trophy, or bragging about some fabulous party her mom—the "big-time Hollywood choreographer"—was taking her to. "You're never in this good of a mood—and frankly, it's freaking me out."

Bria Chang nodded. "The only time I've seen you this happy was when you tripped Rochelle and she fell into the judges' laps at the Soaring Stars competition."

"Don't be ridiculous!" Liberty said in a singsongy voice. "Can't a girl be in a great mood?"

"Sure," Rochelle said, raising an eyebrow. "But the question is *why* are you in a great mood? And which one of us is going to suffer because of it?"

Liberty smoothed her long blond hair back into a neat bun. "You'll see. I promised Miss Toni I wouldn't tell till class."

So there it was! Liberty had a secret.

Rochelle gritted her teeth. "Spill it, Liberty. I hate surprises."

"Oh, but you'll like *this* surprise," Liberty said, batting her eyelashes. "You all will. Ta-ta! See you in the studio."

She grabbed her toe shoes and twirled out of the room, leaving her teammates behind, stunned and confused.

Bria flipped open her laptop notebook. "Something's up. I'm so Googling!"

She typed in Liberty's name, then her mother's: Jane Montgomery.

"Anything?" Scarlett asked anxiously.

Bria scanned through the websites that listed Hollywood gossip and dance news. "Well, Mrs. Montgomery had lunch at the Ivy . . . and she attended New York Fashion Week."

Rochelle rolled her eyes. "I don't care about her mom's social life. I care that she knows something she's not telling us. That is never a good thing."

"Well, I don't see anything that would make

Liberty so weirdly happy—unless her mom picked up some couture costume off the runway for her."

Rochelle doubted it was that. "Liberty loves clothes—but not enough to rub our faces in it. Whatever it is, it's BIG."

Scarlett glanced at the clock. "There's only one way to find out—we gotta get to class."

When the girls entered the studio, their dance coach, Antoinette Moore, was also smiling. And Miss Toni practically *never* smiled.

"Okay, this is creepy," Rochelle whispered. "I feel like I'm in a nightmare or a scary movie: *Horror in the Dance Studio.* Someone pinch me and wake me up."

Instead, Scarlett dragged her over to the ballet *barre*. "Let's not jump to conclusions," she told her friend.

"Maybe Mrs. Montgomery is buying Dance Divas Studio as a present for Liberty," Bria suggested.

"I doubt that would make Miss Toni happy," said Anya Bazarov, their other teammate . . . She'd gotten to the studio earlier and overheard part of the conversation between Liberty and their coach while she was warming up. "All I know is that Liberty told her something and Toni hugged her."

"Toni hugged her?" Rochelle gasped. "It's worse than we thought!"

The door burst open and Gracie, Scarlett's seven-year-old little sister, raced in. "I'm here!" she said breathlessly. "Sorry, Miss Toni. I got bubble gum on my shoe and it made it all sticky." She held up the bottom of her ballet slipper to show off the wad of pink gum.

The girls giggled. Little Gracie was an amazing gymnast, but she had a knack for getting herself into messes!

Toni hated tardiness—and stepping in gum was no excuse. But it didn't seem to bother her today.

"Let me have that, Gracie," Toni said, extending her hand for the ballet slipper. She scraped the gum off with the back of a pen. "Watch where you're walking next time." She winked.

"As for the rest of you . . . ," she began.

"Oh, boy. Here it comes." Rochelle closed her eyes tightly and waited for the bomb to drop.

"I have some amazing news," Toni continued, "which I think I will let Liberty share with you."

Liberty stepped in front of the class. "So, you all know how my mom is a famous Hollywood choreographer who's worked with Katy Perry, Beyoncé, Britney . . ."

Rochelle elbowed Scarlett. Now this was more like it. Liberty was back to bragging.

"Well, she's working with this hot girl group called the Sugar Dolls—there's Candy Doll, Sporty Doll, Baby Doll, Jazzy Doll, and Rag Doll."

Rochelle raised her hand. "And this has to do with us how?"

Miss Toni frowned. "Rochelle, let Liberty finish."

"Thank you, Miss Toni," Liberty said. "So the Sugar Dolls are shooting a video in Hollywood, and they need backup dancers. That's where we come in."

Bria's eyes grew wide. "You mean we're going to be in a music video? Seriously?"

Toni nodded. "Yes, Jane called me last night and asked if we had time to fly out to California. There's a dance competition there in two weeks, so I don't see why we couldn't compete and then stay to shoot the video. It would be a great opportunity to get the Divas' name out there."

"Woo-hoo!" Rochelle shouted. "We're going to Hollywood!"

"There's just one little, itty-bitty thing," Liberty said, interrupting the celebration. "There's, of course, a lead backup dancer who will get a solo."

Everyone was silent except for Gracie. "Ooh! Can I be it?" she said, waving her hand in Liberty's face. Gracie had stage fright most of the time she had to perform in front of a live audience—but not camera fright. "I really, really want to be on TV!"

"Unfortunately, that is not my decision," Toni

explained. "Jane is going to audition all of you, and she'll choose the girl who gets the solo in the video."

"And we all know who that will be," Rochelle said, glaring at Liberty. "We don't stand a chance."

Toni clapped her hands, meaning it was back to business. "Okay, so we have our work cut out for us. We have a major competition and a music video to shoot, and just two short weeks to prepare for both."

Liberty stretched her leg on the *barre*. "Some of us are already prepared," she said, smirking.

"Some of us already have an in with the choreographer," Rochelle said, correcting her.

Toni shushed them. "No talking! Anyone who doesn't give me one hundred ten percent in this competition is not shooting the video. Is that clear?"

Gracie's hand shot up again. "I'm learning percentages in school, and it's only one hundred percent for a whole pie."

Toni tried not to smile. "Thank you for the

math correction, Gracie," she said. "Point taken. What I mean to say is that I want you to give it your all."

If there was one thing Dance Divas knew how to do, it was give it their all—especially when Hollywood was calling.

CHAPTER 2

Hooray for Hollywood

At their rehearsal, Miss Toni rolled in a TV and a DVD player.

"Anyone got popcorn?" Rochelle joked. "Maybe Milk Duds?"

"I hope it's *Brave*," Scarlett whispered. "That's my fave movie."

Miss Toni hit Play and an old black-and-white silent film popped up.

Bria looked confused. There was no talking, just some twinkly piano music on the sound track. "Nope, that's not *Brave*."

"This gentleman is Charlie Chaplin," Toni

explained, pointing to a short actor with a mustache, bowler hat, and cane. "He is my inspiration for our group number at the Electric Dance competition in L.A."

The girls watched as he pierced two potatoes with forks and pretended to do a "table ballet."

"That is so funny!" Gracie giggled. "I like him!"

"Good!" Toni said. "Because you are all going to play him in our group routine. I call it 'Listen Up.'"

Anya raised her hand. "I thought you said Charlie Chaplin made silent films. How can you listen if there's nothing to listen to?"

"You speak with your body—Chaplin always did," Toni explained. "Every movement means something." She motioned for Bria to stand up. "Come. Let me show you."

Bria stood up nervously. Miss Toni always made her jittery when she asked her to demonstrate.

"Bria," she instructed, "walk like this." She hit a button on the DVD player, and Charlie Chaplin showed up again, waddling around, twirling his cane in the air. "Turn your feet out. Wider! Now shuffle."

Bria tried to do as Toni said, but she felt stiff and awkward. Her teacher tossed her a black bowler hat and a wicker cane. "This might help." Then she handed her a costume: a pair of baggy pants and a suit jacket.

"The character Charlie played is called 'the Little Tramp,'" Toni added. "He doesn't have a lot of money, and he bumbles along through life."

Liberty glanced at Rochelle. "Sound like anyone you know, Rock?"

"But he has a heart of gold," Toni continued, "and he always tries to behave like a gentleman." She turned to Bria. "I know that's a lot to take in, but I think you're a good actress. I think you can connect with this character."

Bria looked at herself in the studio mirrors.

She looked ridiculous! The jacket was way too small—the buttons were popping open—and the pants were huge. "Oh! Almost forgot!" Toni said. She brought out an oversize pair of men's shoes. "Put these on."

"How am I supposed to dance in those?" Bria whined.

"Chaplin did." Toni helped her into the clown-like loafers. "Now walk," she commanded.

Bria stepped forward, trying to mimic the moves she had seen on the DVD. "Bob your head side to side, shoulders back, chin up," Toni barked. "Keep the legs stiff. Think of a penguin, but with more flair and musicality."

Slowly, Briana began to walk. She tipped her hat, twirled her cane, and pointed her feet out to the sides.

"Wow! Bri, that is amazing!" Scarlett said. "You got it!"

"I second that," Toni said. "And that's how I want to see you all do it. The music is going to be a simple piano tune—fast, then slow, then fast again. The facial gestures have to be larger than life. And I'm going to project a silent film on a giant screen behind you while a strobe light flashes so you'll look like you're moving in slow motion."

Liberty's hand went up. "And are there going to be any solos in the competition? Just askin'."

"As if," Rochelle muttered under her breath. "Just askin' to have one!"

Toni tapped her ballet shoe on the floor. "I have given that some thought," she said. "There'll be two solos, a duet, and our showstopping group routine."

She walked over to Scarlett and handed her a blond wig. "You'll be Marilyn Monroe in a number called 'Breakable.'"

"Hey!" Liberty protested. "I have *naturally* blond hair! And I'm naturally glamorous! Why can't I be Marilyn?"

Toni walked over and presented her with a cowboy hat.

"What's this?" Liberty asked. She didn't look thrilled.

"You and Bria are doing a country-inspired acro routine."

Liberty fumed. "Seriously? She gets to be Marilyn and I get to be . . . home on the range?"

"Where the deer and the antelope play," Bria pointed out, giggling.

Miss Toni continued: "And Rochelle. I don't have a costume for you, yet."

"Why? You're not gonna wrap me in toilet paper or tin foil or something weird like that?" she asked nervously. She would never forget the time Toni dressed her up like a hot dog and made her dance a contemporary routine to "Who Let the Dogs Out?"

"No—but thanks for the idea! I'll take it into consideration." Toni smirked. "You're going to play a kid arriving in Hollywood, hoping to see her name in lights one day. I call the number 'Rising Star,' and it has hip-hop in it. So you can say, 'Thank you, Miss Toni.'"

"Awesome!" Rochelle cheered. "I mean, thanks, Miss Toni!" Her teacher knew hip-hop was her favorite style of dance, which was probably why she rarely let Rochelle perform it in a competition. She believed in challenging the Divas and pushing them out of their comfort zones.

"So that should be all for today," Toni said. "I want everyone here on time tomorrow, ready to work. This is going to be a tough competition. Not only are the best dance teams in California competing, but I hear City Feet is making the trip as well."

"Oh my gooshness," Gracie exclaimed. "Not again!"

Bria agreed with her. The very mention of their name made her skin crawl. No matter how many times the Divas beat them (and they had many times), just being in the same auditorium with those girls—Mandy, Regan, Phoebe, and Addison—set them *all* on edge.

"Never mind City Feet," Toni warned them. "Just worry about yourselves. And remember what

Chaplin said: 'You'll never find a rainbow if you're looking down.'"

She left the girls to gather their bags. "We might not find a rainbow, but we'll find City Feet," Rochelle said. "If there's one thing they like to do, it's to play down and dirty."

CHAPTER 3

These Boots Were Made for Dancing

When Bria showed up to rehearse her duet with Liberty on Tuesday night, she never expected to see her partner dressed like a rhinestone cowboy.

"Whaddaya think?" Liberty said, modeling a gold sequin vest and shorts over a white leotard. "Taylor Swift's costume designer made it for me." She plopped a gold sequin cowboy hat on her head and tied on a white satin mask. "Too much? You think I should lose the mask?"

Bria was speechless. "No, I think the mask is fine . . . It's the rest of the outfit I'm worried about."

Miss Toni walked in the studio and dropped her clipboard. Her mouth hung open. "What in heaven's name are you dressed for? Halloween?" she boomed. "This is supposed to be set in the Old West. Not Las Vegas!"

"I just thought . . . ," Liberty started to explain.

"Don't think. Just change. Now!"

As Liberty ran to the dressing room, Bria stared at the clock on the wall. It was already 6:00 p.m., and she had a ton of homework and a science quiz tomorrow.

"Am I keeping you?" Toni asked.

Bria shook her head. "No, Miss Toni. I just have a lot of studying to do."

Toni perched on her stool. "Your mom tells me you're an excellent student, Bria," she said. "So why are you worried?"

Bria sighed. What she wanted to tell her dance coach was how much pressure she felt in her family to do well. Her dad was a journalist, and her sister was a genius. That left her to keep up—which she barely managed to do with fifteen hours a week of dance class and rehearsals. Her mom insisted she maintain a B+ average or she couldn't be a Diva. She *really* wanted Miss Toni to understand what she went through, day after day.

Instead, she simply answered, "I'm okay."

Finally, Liberty returned, dressed in a simple black leotard and cowboy boots.

"Much better," Toni commented. "No costume designers. I'll be providing your look for this duet."

Liberty rolled her eyes. If it was an "Old West" style, then it was bound to be sequin-less.

Miss Toni hit a button on her MP3 player and a song boomed over the speaker. "This is a high-energy routine," she told them. "I want the moves strong and staccato. I want to see a clean barrel jump, Liberty. And Bria, watch those arms in the axle turn. They've been looking like linguini!"

At the end of the routine, they were both supposed to climb into their saddles mounted in the middle of the stage and yell, "Hi-ho, Silver! Away!" For now, they swung their legs over a chair back.

"We're lucky she didn't make us ride a mechanical bull," Liberty whispered to Bria.

"I heard that!" Toni shouted. Her back was turned, and the music was blaring, but she never missed a comment—especially a snarky one. "And thank you for the wonderful idea, Liberty. I do think we should have the saddles move up and down—as if you're riding into the sunset on your trusty steeds."

"But I was kidding!" Liberty exclaimed. "And what's a steed?"

"A horse," Bria replied. She wondered if Liberty ever used her head.

"Well, I'm not kidding," Toni said. "It's an extra surprise that the judges will never see coming."

"It's an added surprise I didn't see coming," Bria said, elbowing her duet partner. "Thanks a lot, Liberty!"

Liberty crossed her hands over her chest. "Look, it's not my fault. I wanted this routine to be glam, not grunge. I was even having my costume designer make you something."

"Thanks," Bria said. "I think."

Toni waved her hand in the air. "Enough! You're dismissed. I've had enough horsing around for today."

"How'd it go?" Scarlett asked Liberty and Bria as they flopped down on benches in the dressing room.

"You mean how *didn't* it go?" Liberty said grumpily. "Toni totally shot down my couture cowboy costume."

"But she did approve your idea for the rocking horses," Bria complained. "Did I mention I have no idea how to ride a horse?"

"A horse? Seriously?" Scarlett chuckled. "How are we gonna fit that in the overhead on our flight to L.A.?"

"Not a real horse—a mechanical one. That goes up and down," Bria said. "Did I also mention I get motion sickness, Liberty?"

"She does," Scarlett said, nodding. "Trust me. I sat next to her on the Tilt-A-Whirl at the spring carnival and it was not pretty."

"Just thinking about it makes me queasy," Bria said, sighing.

"Oh, stop complaining," Liberty said. "The horse is the least of our problems. Our costumes are going to be totally drab and probably covered in dust and tumbleweeds."

Scarlett tucked her hair under a glamorous blond wig. "How do I look?"

Liberty frowned. "That just makes me feel worse. I hate this duet! I hate Miss Toni! The Marilyn Monroe solo should have been mine."

"Gee, someone's in a bad mood. That's more like it," Rochelle said, striding into the dressing room. "I feel so much better when Liberty is miserable."

"For your information, I am not *miserable*,"

she insisted. "Actually, when I think about it, I'm thrilled. I spoke to my mom this morning and she says I'm a shoo-in for the spotlight dancer in the Sugar Dolls' video."

"Aw, that's so nice of your mommy to give you the lead," Rochelle replied. "It must be nice to be a spoiled brat who gets whatever she wants."

"And it must be nice to be talentless *and* clueless," Liberty shot back.

"Divas! Divas!" Scarlett stepped in to referee. "Can we focus on the positive here? We're all going to Hollywood! We're all going to be in a pop video."

Liberty shot Rochelle a nasty look. "Not if I can help it. I'm calling my mom right now." She stormed out of the room.

"You think she's bluffing?" Bria asked Rochelle.

"Don't know, don't care." Rochelle shrugged. "When I'm a pro dancer, I'm gonna be cast in a ton of music videos. I don't need Liberty Montgomery to do me any favors."

"But, Rock, I want you to be in the video with

us," Scarlett said. "We're a team. It wouldn't be any fun without you."

"Just say you're sorry for calling her a spoiled brat," Bria suggested.

"But she *is* a spoiled brat," Rochelle said.

"Rock, please?" Scarlett pleaded. "For me?"

Rochelle sighed. "Fine. I'll go find Liberty and tell her I'm sorry. But I'm crossing my fingers behind my back."

Scarlett looked at Bria and shook her head. "Maybe we should rename our team the Drama Divas?"

CHAPTER 4

Toe Shoes Are a Girl's Best Friend

"The style of your solo is classical ballet," Miss Toni explained to Scarlett on Wednesday. "Marilyn was a beautiful, tragic figure. I want you to dance *en pointe* and make the judges fall in love with you."

"My mom said she was a bombshell—whatever that means," Scarlett said, stretching at the *barre*.

"It means she was vivacious and people tripped over themselves just to get near her," Toni explained. "She seemed sweet and innocent, even naive at times. But she wielded a tremendous amount of power."

Scarlett fastened the ribbons on her toe shoes. "That's a lot of different things to show in one dance," she said.

"If anyone can do it, you can," Toni said. "I'm counting on you. Don't let me down."

Scarlett loved how much faith Miss Toni had in her, but at the same time, it made her nervous. What if she missed a step? Tripped and fell? It had all happened before, and she knew it would happen again. She just hoped it wasn't at Electric Dance.

"The arms and legs have to balance each other out," she said while she demonstrated. "I want long and graceful mixed with strength." She did a perfect *tombé pas de bourrée* and then a *pirouette* into a finishing fourth. It took Scarlett's breath away. Sometimes she forgot that Miss Toni had once been a prima ballerina. She and Justine Chase, City Feet's coach, had been students together at American Ballet Company, where their friendship had begun and ended. But why it ended was still a puzzle. The girls had learned that Justine tried to steal Toni's roles and even her boyfriend. But they also suspected there had to be more to the story. The only thing that was clear was that Miss Toni wanted to beat City Feet just as much as the Divas did—maybe even more. For her, it was personal.

"This will be your costume." Miss Toni pulled a silky white halter dress out of the closet. "Very Marilyn, don't you think?"

Scarlett nodded. She especially loved the tiny pearls around the neckline and waist. It was both delicate and glam at the same time—exactly how she imagined Marilyn Monroe had been.

"The key will be to keep it real," Miss Toni said, adjusting Scarlett's turnout. "Nothing over the top. Just clean, beautiful lines and a haunted face. Let me see it."

Scarlett tried to look both pained and pretty at the same time. She pouted her lips and blinked her eyes.

"Oh no . . . You look like a puppy dog!" Toni complained. "You need to practice in front of a mirror. If you make that face, there is no way you're taking home first place in Junior Solo. The judges will throw you a dog biscuit!"

Scarlett winced. Sometimes Toni's critiques stung. But she nodded her head and promised she'd work on it.

"Scoot then, Scoot," Toni said. "Isn't that what Gracie calls you?"

Scarlett rolled her eyes. "Yeah, unfortunately."

"Well, I'm going to call you 'Sour Puss' until I see a better Marilyn face."

*   *
  *

At home that night, Scarlett stood in front of her bathroom mirror, trying to channel her inner Marilyn.

"What are you doing?" Gracie asked, watching her make strange faces at her reflection.

"Do you mind? I'm working on showing emotion for my solo at Electric Dance."

Gracie looked confused. "Are you supposed to be sick?"

"No!" Scarlett shot back. "I'm supposed to be sad and tragic and incredibly beautiful."

Gracie shook her head. "You look like you have a tummy ache."

Scarlett tried another face: this one with a furrowed brow and a wrinkled nose.

"Yup," Gracie said. "That's definitely the ouchy face."

"Mom!" Scarlett shouted. "Gracie is driving me crazy!"

"Am not!" Gracie replied. "I'm trying to help!"

Scarlett shooed her away and went to her room, where she brought up video chat on her computer. Bria appeared on the other end.

"I knew you'd be on your computer!" Scarlett said. Bria was always up late, studying one subject or another.

"Make it quick." She sighed. "I have twenty more problems to go on my pre-algebra homework."

"I can't get the right face for my solo," Scarlett explained. "I can feel it when I dance, but I just can't get that feeling from my toes to my head."

Bria thought for a moment. "Imagine yourself dancing on the stage. Now try."

Scarlett made a face into the computer camera. "How's this?"

"You kind of look like you ate one of Gracie's crazy recipes and you have a stomachache," Bria said.

"Miss Toni said she wants my face to look haunted. But apparently all I can do is look sick."

"I think the problem is that you're trying too hard," Bria suggested. "Don't pretend. Think of something really sad and connect with it."

Scarlett racked her brain for the saddest memory she could think of. "I just don't know," she told her friend. "What would you say is your saddest memory?"

"Definitely my last science pop quiz," Bria said. "That was a nightmare. I blanked and forgot all the answers."

"No, I mean something really, *really* sad. Something that breaks your heart," Scarlett insisted. Then it came to her: the day, two years ago, that her mom and dad told her they were getting divorced.

"Please! Don't!" she had screamed at her parents through hysterical tears. "I don't want this to happen to us."

"Honey." Her dad had tried to calm her. "You have to be a big girl about this. It's not working between your mom and me, and we can't live together anymore."

"We'll always be here for you and Gracie," her mom added. "We love you and your sister so much, and nothing will ever change that."

Scarlett remembered feeling like someone had knocked the wind out of her. She felt completely lost and helpless. There was nothing she could do to keep their family together. It felt like floating aimlessly in space, with no one and nothing to grab on to . . .

"That's it, that's it!" Bria shouted, snapping her friend back to the present day. "Scarlett, that was a great face."

Scarlett shuddered and shook the feeling away.

"I guess that's what I need to think about," she said. "Poor Marilyn. I can't imagine feeling like that all the time."

"Well, just remember it for your next rehearsal," Bria said. "And if it doesn't work, I can give you my science quiz. It's pretty sad and scary."

CHAPTER 5

Hip-Hop to It

Rochelle showed up for her solo rehearsal ten minutes early. She figured it couldn't hurt to get on Miss Toni's good side, especially since she had yet to design her costume.

"Well, look who's here!" Toni said, entering the studio. "I guess the key to getting you to come to class on time is to give you a hip-hop number."

"Yeah, well, I'm really psyched for it," Rochelle said, shuffling her feet on the ground.

"Good. Because I have a special surprise for you."

Rochelle's eyes lit up. "Am I going to dance

with Hayden Finley again?" For the Leaps and Bounds competition, Toni had paired her with a boy, and they'd been hanging out together ever since.

Toni shook her head. "Nope. You and Hayden will have to do your partnering out of the studio," she said firmly. There was no putting anything past her dance coach. She knew that she and Hayden liked each other—despite the fact that Rochelle had hurt her ankle and messed up their chance to dance together in the competition.

"No duet this time. This one is all yours," Toni said. "If you think you're up to it."

Rochelle nodded. "Oh yeah. Bring it on!"

The door of the studio cracked open. "Hey, y'all!" called a deep voice.

"Come in!" Toni replied. "Rochelle, I'd like you to meet Jerome."

"So this is the famous Rochelle I've heard about," the man said as he entered the studio. He was wearing the coolest outfit Rochelle had ever seen: black pants and a colorful graphic tee with a black leather jacket over it. "Nice to meet you."

"It's Rock," Rochelle answered, extending her hand to shake.

The man grinned. "Your name says it all. You can call me J. J."

"J. J. has a fine reputation as a hip-hop choreographer," Toni explained. "And since that kind of dance is not my specialty, I thought I'd bring in someone to help you really bust some moves."

J. J. smiled. "I don't know the first thing about dancing on my toes. But I do know some pretty smooth moves."

He demonstrated a quick pop and lock and drop it. "I figured we'd mix up some new moves with old school," he said. "Keep the judges guessing."

"As long as you keep the judges smiling," Toni warned him. "I want a winning routine."

J. J. tipped his baseball cap. "Yes, ma'am!" he said with a wink. "Is she always this pushy, Rock?"

Rock almost said "you better believe it!"—but

thought twice since Miss Toni was staring at her. "Miss Toni isn't pushy. She's just got strong opinions."

"And I have not formed an opinion yet about this routine," she fired back. "So wow me, J. J.—and you, too, Rochelle."

* * *

For two hours, J. J. put Rochelle through her paces. It was a very complicated routine done to a rapid-fire rap song. "Keep on the rhythm," he yelled. "You're falling behind the beat. Faster! Faster! Stop being lazy and dragging your feet. I want an explosion. I want to see attitude!"

When she came out of the studio, she was exhausted and dripping sweat. She could barely crawl back to the dressing room.

"I feel like I've been through a war," she panted, collapsing on the bench.

Scarlett tossed her a towel. "I guess the new choreographer Miss Toni hired is tough?"

"Tough?" Rochelle sat up and mopped her

face with the towel. "He's like the guy version of Toni! He's scary tough."

"I think he's really nice," Gracie interjected.

"How do you know?" Rochelle asked her.

"'Cause when I got here after school, Miss Toni introduced me to him."

"I met him, too," Anya piped up. "He seems really cool."

Rochelle shook her head. "I am in serious trouble."

"Not as much trouble as I am," Bria said suddenly. She was staring in disbelief at her laptop screen. "They just posted our grades for the science midterm!"

Rochelle sighed. "You know, you worry way too much, Bri. You studied like a maniac, and I'm sure you knocked it out of the park."

Bria turned the laptop around to show them what it said. There, in big red type, was the letter "F."

"You failed it?" Scarlett gasped. "How? Why?"

"I have no idea!" Bria cried. "All I know is

that my parents are gonna kill me. And there goes the trip to Hollywood. They'll never let me go now."

"Maybe you can do some extra credit," Gracie volunteered. "Like a diorama or a poster or something."

"That might work in second grade, Gracie, but my science teacher, Ms. Moran, doesn't believe in extra credit." Bria buried her head in her hands. "I'm doomed. Doomed, doomed, doomed."

"I actually think Gracie had a great idea," Scarlett said.

"I did?" Gracie replied. "I mean, I did! What did I say?"

"You said Bria should do some extra credit—and I think that's exactly what she should do." Scarlett turned to Bria. "Just like how you wow those tough judges every competition, you can wow your teacher, too."

"How?" Bria sighed. "She won't appreciate my back handspring."

"No, but she will appreciate it if you rap the entire science unit and prove that you know it."

"Rap? I don't rap," Bria replied.

"Which is exactly why we're going to teach you how. And we'll all do a routine as your backup dancers," Scarlett said, nodding to all of the girls.

Anya held up her hand. "I don't get it. We're going to drag her science teacher here to the studio to watch us do a number?"

"Nope!" Scarlett replied. "Bria is going to make a video on her laptop and bring it to school."

"Like a real music video?" Gracie asked. "Like Lady Gaga?"

"Better," Scarlett said, smiling. "Lady Bria!"

"I can definitely help," Rochelle said. "As soon as I catch my breath."

Bria sighed. It was a long shot. But it was either this or be grounded for all eternity and miss out on going to Hollywood. "Okay, I'll try anything to get Ms. Moran to give me a better grade."

Anya peeked outside of the dressing room. "Studio three is empty. And I think we could sneak in and pull down the shades so Miss Toni won't see us."

Rochelle wiped the sweat off her forehead and scooped her long curls into a messy bun. "Let's see what we're dealing with," she said, turning Bria's laptop toward her. She studied the screen. "Earth Science? Worms? You want Bria to rap this?" she said to Scarlett.

"I told you it's hopeless," Bria said. "I can't think of anything that rhymes with protozoa."

"I don't know-a!" Gracie said, giggling. "That rhymes!"

Scarlett scratched her head. "Well, it would have been easier if it was biology. 'The leg bone's connected to the hip bone' kind of stuff. But I'm not giving up yet."

Liberty swept into the dressing room—and Rochelle quickly covered Bria's laptop with her towel.

"What are you guys up to?" she asked.

"We're making a music vid—" Gracie started to say before Scarlett clamped a hand over her mouth.

"Oh, nothing," Scarlett fibbed. The last thing they needed was for Liberty to butt in on Bria's extra credit project. "Just homework."

Liberty looked from face to face. "Homework? Are you sure?" She turned to Gracie. "Or are you hiding something?"

Gracie bit her lip. "Nuh-uh. We're helping Bria with her science homework." Technically, it wasn't a lie.

Liberty grabbed her dance bag off the shelf and glanced over her shoulder. "Okay, if you're all going to sit here and do homework, I'm outta here. I have much more exciting things to do."

"I bet," Rochelle muttered. "Ta-ta, Liberty!" She waved her off.

Once the coast was clear, they uncovered Bria's computer again and began planning. "So worms eat bacteria, fungi, protozoa, organic matter, and decaying animals?"

"*Eww!*" Anya squirmed. "That's disgusting."

"Tell me about it," Bria groaned. "This is why I failed my test. It grosses me out."

Rochelle hopped off the bench and began to wiggle her hips. "*Do the worm, do the worm,*" she began to rap. "*Shimmy up, shimmy down, spin yourself around. Crawl through the soil, slink through the ground.*" She got on her stomach and rested the palms of her hands parallel to her chest on the floor. Then she began to kick her legs in the air and the rest of her body popped up in a wiggly motion.

"Go Rock! Go Rock!" the girls chanted. "Do the worm dance! Do the worm dance!"

Bria continued to write the rap. "*A worm is the coolest—and that's no lie. He sucks up his food in the blink of an eye. Be it teeny-tiny things or a bird that's dead, he grinds them in his gizzard—you heard what I said!*"

"OMG, that's hilarious!" Scarlett giggled. "Bria, you can totally do this! I think we're ready to go shoot it."

They tiptoed into studio 3, and Bria set her computer on a stool to film. Rochelle handed her a piece of paper. "Here's the rest of it. Now make sure you give it attitude—and a beat."

"*An earthworm has no eyes to see; it picks up the vibe from you and me. It feels that vibe along the ground, and it senses bright light all around,*" Bria read.

"Again! With more 'tude!" Rochelle instructed her.

"You sound like Miss Toni." Gracie giggled. "Very tossy!"

"Tossy?" Rochelle looked to Scarlett for a translation. Her little sis was always making up her own Gracie language.

"Tossy. Tough plus bossy," Scarlett explained. "It's a compliment."

"Oh, then thanks, Gracie," Rochelle said. "I think."

Just then, there was a knock on the studio door. "Quick!" Bria shouted, slamming her laptop shut. "It must be Miss Toni. Everyone act like we're rehearsing the group number."

The girls raced to the center of the room and

got into position as the door creaked open. It was J. J.

"Who's he?" Anya whispered.

"My tossy new choreographer—aka Miss Toni's boyfriend," Rochelle explained.

"So, what's up in here?" he asked. "Do I sense some trouble brewing?"

Rochelle stepped forward. "No, no trouble. Just rehearsal for our group number." To drive the point home, she waddled like Charlie Chaplin.

J. J. nodded and took a seat on the floor. "Great. Let's see it."

"See it?" Scarlett gasped. "You mean now?"

"Yeah. Just go on with what you were all doing. Don't mind me. I'll just be a fly on the wall."

Bria shrugged. It was no use trying to hide what they were up to. "We're not actually rehearsing the group number," she confessed. "Everyone was just helping me do an extra-credit science project on earthworms."

J. J. nodded. "So that's why I saw you all do a pretty poor imitation of the worm dance?"

Rochelle rested her hands on her hips. Of

course, he had been spying on them through the crack in the door! "It was not a poor imitation. I choreographed it."

J. J. chuckled. He dropped down on the floor and began "worming" across it. "See how the body ripples? You want to keep the arms and elbows strong and let the rest be fluid. Pop up, flow down, pop up, flow down . . ."

Scarlett elbowed Rochelle. "He does do a good worm."

"Fine. Thanks for showing us," Rochelle said.

"Let me see what else you got," J. J. said, jumping to his feet. "Maybe I can help you refine it."

"That would be so nice of you!" Bria exclaimed.

"We got it under control," Rochelle countered. "Thanks."

J. J. raised an eyebrow. "You sure? You wouldn't want the choreographer who did Justin Timberlake's last concert gig to lend you a hand?"

"JT?" Anya gasped. "I love him! That is so amazing!"

Rochelle rolled her eyes. "We wouldn't want JT's choreographer ratting us out to Miss Toni."

J. J. grinned. "I see. So I'm a spy, is that it?"

Rochelle shrugged. "You said it. Not us."

"Well, what if I promised not to breathe a word to your dance teacher? I can keep a secret." He pretended to lock up his lips and throw away the key.

"I think we can trust him," Bria said quietly. "He seems really nice."

Rochelle shrugged.

J. J. paced the studio floor. "So you really wanna impress this science teacher, right?"

Bria nodded. "Totally! I need at least a B plus or my mom will never let me go to Hollywood."

"Then, I say make it authentic. You won't find any earthworms rolling around Miss Toni's squeaky-clean dance studio. You need dirt."

Gracie jumped up and down. "I love dirt! Do we get to roll in the dirt?"

"I think you should take this shoot out back behind the studio. That way you can get down *and* dirty . . . You know what I'm saying?"

"It's a really good idea, Bria," Scarlett piped up. "We can shoot some close-ups of the grass and maybe even find some real worms."

"In dance and life, authenticity is everything," J. J. added. "I'm happy to record it for you on my phone. And we can add a pretty decent beat box."

Bria grabbed Rochelle by the arm and tugged. "Come on, guys! What are we waiting for? Let's get wiggling!"

CHAPTER 6

A Little Help from My Friends

The Divas filed out behind the studio. "This is an awesome spot," Bria declared, smudging soil across her cheeks and forehead. "Who knew? We never get outside the studio!"

Anya agreed, jumping in a huge pile of crunchy, colorful fall leaves. "In L.A., we never get to see the leaves change like this. I'm lovin' this!"

J. J. whistled through his teeth to get their attention. "Okay, let's focus. Rub some dirt on your faces, your leotards, your tights. Worms are not clean, so let me see it."

They shot for over two hours, creating a grand

finale where Bria rolled down a hill and landed in a pile of leaves.

She stood up, faced the camera and rapped: *"Worms eat food scraps—so I'm your friend. It passes through my body and out my tail end. This compost is used to grow plants—so true! They call it 'vermicompost' and it looks like goo!"*

"EWWW!" the rest of the Divas screamed in the background. Then they raced down the hill and tackled each other.

"Okay! That's a wrap!" J. J. called. "Nice job, girls."

Bria was laughing so hard she could barely catch her breath. She had leaves in her hair and dirt all over her face. "That was amazing. Thanks, everyone. I'm going to do the edit tonight and show Ms. Moran in the morning. Cross your fingers she likes it!"

Scarlett held up her hand with her fingers crossed. Then she caught a glimpse of her watch.

"Guys, it's six twenty! We're twenty minutes late for group rehearsal. Miss Toni is gonna kill us!"

They raced back inside and directly into

studio 2, where Miss Toni was already rehearsing with Liberty.

Rochelle took a deep breath and braced herself. She knew this wasn't going to be pretty.

Toni spun around and stared. For the first time since they'd known her, the Divas' dance coach was completely speechless.

"OMG!" Liberty gasped. "Did you guys go mud wrestling?"

Bria thought quickly. "No, we were actually practicing out back. Um, you know, the Little Tramp and all . . ."

Scarlett picked up where she left off. "Right! We were just getting into character." She smudged some dirt across her upper lip to look like a mustache. "See?"

Toni still looked stunned. "Rochelle, do you have anything to add to this?" she finally asked.

"Um, well, in dance and life, authenticity is everything," she replied.

Toni raised an eyebrow. "Was J. J. perhaps involved in your authentic Little Tramp rehearsal?"

Gracie smiled. "How'd ya know?"

Toni put down her clipboard and marched toward the door. She looked furious. "I'm going to have a few words with him. In the meantime, I expect you all to clean up yourselves, then my dance studio floor." She pointed to the black smudges and piles of dirt they'd scattered around.

"Uh-oh," Gracie said. "J. J. is in trouble!"

Miss Toni still wasn't back by the time they'd washed up, put on new leotards and tights, and returned to the studio.

"Do you think she's gonna fire him?" Bria whispered.

"Miss Toni's been mad at me tons of times and she always gets over it," Rochelle said.

Apparently, she was right. The door opened and J. J. walked inside.

"So," he began, "Miss Toni has asked me to take over the rehearsal for tonight."

Scarlett raised her hand. "How come?"

"I'm not really sure," J. J. answered. "Something

about 'having to connect more with the material.' She went off to do some research, I guess."

"This is all my fault," Bria said, staring down at the floor. "I made Miss Toni mad at us."

"You want my advice?" J. J. asked. "I think you should just nail your routine and let Miss Toni cool down."

Rochelle bristled. "We took your advice before and look where it got us!"

"We don't really have any other choice," Anya pointed out. "The competition is two weeks away and we don't even know the whole choreography."

"Exactly!" J. J. said, studying Toni's notes. "So let's clean up those *jetés* before she comes back."

"*Jetés?* What do you know about *jetés?*" Rochelle asked. "I thought you didn't know anything about ballet."

"I guess Toni's rubbing off on me," he said with a wink. "Let's take it from the top."

The next day, Bria came to school an hour early to meet with her science teacher. She could hardly sleep, she was so nervous.

"Bria?" Ms. Moran asked. "What are you doing here so early?"

"I um . . . I . . . well . . . ," Bria stuttered.

"This has to do with your test grade, doesn't it?" her teacher said, sighing. "I tried calling you at home last night, but your mom said you were at your dance class."

"I know. I'm sorry. But let me show you something!" Bria pleaded. She opened her laptop and the worm video started playing. Ms. Moran watched it intently. "I can't believe you did this," she said.

"I did. I really did!" Bria said. "I do know the material, I swear! I just panicked on the test. I'm not sure what went wrong."

"I know what went wrong," Ms. Moran assured her. "There was a computer error. When I saw the F, I knew something was wrong. I went back and marked your test again by hand. I changed your grade last night. You didn't fail, Bria. You got an A minus."

Bria's eyes lit up. "I did? I didn't fail?"

"No, you didn't fail. But I do think I'll have to change your grade again."

Oh no. Bria's mind began to race. Her teacher hated the video. Now she really *was* going to fail her.

"Please," Bria said. "Can I do it again? I promise I'll do better next time."

Ms. Moran looked puzzled. "You mean an A plus isn't good enough for you?"

"An A plus?" Bria gasped. "Really?"

"Anyone who goes to this much effort to show me she understands earthworms deserves it. My favorite part was the compost goo. Do you mind if I use this for future classes?"

Bria couldn't wait to get to the studio to tell her friends the great news.

＊ ＊
＊

When Bria arrived a few minutes before class started, the dressing room was surprisingly missing all the Divas. So she changed into her leotard and went to look for them. There was a large note on the studio door in Miss Toni's handwriting: Diva Competition Team: Please meet at 111 Alton Street.

"Need a ride?" a voice asked. It was J. J.

"Where are we going?" Bria replied. "And where is everybody?"

"Toni decided to take you girls on a little field trip today. The rest of the gang is there already, but Miss Toni asked me to stay behind and give you a ride when you arrived. We better hurry. Food's getting cold."

"Food?" Bria asked, grabbing her bag and trailing after him to the parking lot.

J. J. nodded and opened the car door. "Yup. You'll see." He made the lock-and-key movements over his lips again. "Miss Toni swore me to secrecy."

CHAPTER 7

Giving Back

J. J. and Bria pulled up in front of a large church with stained-glass windows. Bria noticed there was a long line of people out front. "What are they waiting for?" she said.

"They're hungry," J. J. explained. "Come on in."

He led her through a back door of the church, down a flight of stairs, and into a large, bustling kitchen. There, wearing an apron tied around her waist, was Miss Toni.

"Welcome," she said, noticing Bria and J. J. standing in the doorway. "Well, what are you waiting for? An invitation?" She handed them each a tray of chicken and rice. "Take this out there and start serving."

They both obeyed and headed into the dining room, where Scarlett, Rochelle, Gracie, and Anya were all scooping out dinners on plates for the huge crowd. Bria settled in next to Scarlett. "What is this place?" she asked.

"It's a homeless shelter," Scarlett said. "Miss Toni came here yesterday to volunteer all of us."

"It's really sad," Anya whispered. "So many of these people have no homes, no food. Look over there . . ." She pointed to a dark-haired girl about their age, sitting in the corner with her mother.

Bria smiled at her, but the girl looked the other way. "How do people lose their homes?" she asked.

"A lot of different ways." J. J. tried to explain. "Sometimes they lose their jobs and there's no money coming in. Sometimes there's a tragedy that causes them to lose their way."

Bria stared at the girl. She wondered what her story was. She looked like any girl she'd see in school or at the Dance Divas Studio. She liked her pink sparkly sneakers. "I think I'll go bring someone a piece of pie for dessert," she said, taking a plate from Scarlett.

"Hi," she said warmly, bringing the slice over. "I'm Bria."

The girl didn't say anything. She didn't even look up.

"Reese, where are your manners?" her mother said, scolding her. She put down her sewing and held out her hand. "Hello, there. I'm Genevieve—you can call me Jenny. And this quiet girl is Reese."

"I'm not hungry," Reese insisted, pushing the plate of pie away. She turned her back, opened a book, and plugged in her earphones and iPod.

"What are you listening to?" Bria continued. "I love all kinds of music."

Reese held up the screen.

"Oh, Sugar Dolls!" Bria exclaimed. "I love them! I'm going to meet them when I go to L.A."

Reese turned around. "Seriously? You're going to meet them? You're not making that up?"

"Cross my heart," Bria said, making an X over her chest. "I'm on a dance team and we're going to Hollywood to be their backup dancers."

"You don't need any extra girls, do you?" Reese asked. "I took a lot of dance classes—tap, hip-hop, jazz—before . . . well, you know, before we came here."

Bria sensed that Reese wanted to change the subject.

"Show me what you can do," she said, encouraging Reese. Then she took a seat on the floor and did her best Miss Toni impression. She pursed her lips and squinted her eyes so she looked totally focused. "Go on . . . Wow me!" she said with a wink.

"Here? Now?" Reese replied. There were dozens of people in the room.

"Good a time as any," Bria said. "Unless you're chicken?"

Reese rolled up her sleeves. "No one calls me chicken," she said, getting to her feet. She arched her back and held her leg up behind her in a perfect scorpion move.

"Not bad," Bria said, "but can you do this?" She stood up and did a time-step combination, tapping in her sneakers.

"In my sleep!" Reese copied her and finished it off with a "Shuffle Off to Buffalo."

"Okay, I'm impressed," Bria said. "You've got moves."

"Told ya! Can I be in the Sugar Dolls' video now?"

Bria felt terrible; she hadn't meant to mislead her. "I'm so sorry, Reese. There's only room for five girls."

"So you were just doing that . . . to make fun of me?"

"What? No way!" Bria insisted. "You really *are* a good dancer. I just don't make the decisions when it comes to our team."

"Well, who does?" Reese asked.

Bria pointed to Toni, who was dishing out slices of pecan pie. "Our teacher."

"Her? I've seen her here a couple of times now. She's a dance teacher?"

"The best—and the toughest," Bria answered.

"I'm sorry, but it's really hard to get on our dance team."

"Well, maybe another time." Reese tried to hide her disappointment. "I'm really busy anyway." She went back to her seat and opened up a book.

"Can I ask you a question?" Bria said softly.

Reese sighed. "Sure."

"Why did you give up dancing?"

Reese bit her lip. Obviously, it was a sensitive subject. "There's no money anymore for dance lessons. There was a fire in our house. Almost everything was destroyed, and we don't have any insurance to pay for it. So until my mom makes enough money for us to afford a new place and furniture, we have to stay here."

Bria tried to imagine what she was saying. What would happen to her family if there was a fire in their home? She guessed they would go live with her aunt Robbi or with Gram Loraine and Poppy Blake in Connecticut. The Divas would lend her clothes, and if they needed a place to go, Scarlett and her mom would surely take them in.

"But don't you have any family or friends you could stay with?" she asked Reese.

"My mom is the only family I've got. We're a team," Reese added. "I guess I could have stayed with a school friend, but I wanted to be with my mom."

Bria nodded. She understood what it was to be a team, and how important it was to stick by each other through it all.

"I'm really sorry this happened to you, Reese," Bria said. "I hope your mom gets some money soon."

"Me, too," Reese said. "It's really noisy here at night and it makes it hard to study."

Bria noticed the book in her hand. "Oh no. Earth science. That is the worst!"

"Tell me about it," Reese groaned. "Worms totally gross me out."

"Me, too!" Bria smiled. "But I do happen to be a worm expert—if you want a few tips."

Reese thought for a moment. "I guess that would be okay," she said. When it was time to leave, Reese and Bria exchanged school e-mails and promised to stay in touch. "If you get stuck, just e-mail me," Bria said. "The next unit on oceanography is super tough."

Reese nodded. "I will, Bria. Thanks. I mean, for coming over and everything."

* * *

During the entire car ride home, Bria wondered what Reese had meant by "thanks . . . for coming over and everything."

"I don't get it," she told the other Divas. "All I did was talk to her and kinda help her with some homework."

"You did a lot more than that," Toni replied. "You treated her with kindness, compassion, and respect."

"Why wouldn't I?" Bria asked.

"Because not everyone does," Toni insisted. "I wanted you all to come here tonight and see for yourselves what homelessness looks and feels like."

"Why?" Gracie asked. "Did we do something wrong?"

Toni sighed. "No, I did. I went about teaching you the whole Little Tramp routine wrong. When we get back to the studio tonight, I have a whole new choreography to teach you," Toni said. "We're going to give those judges and that audience a lot to think about."

CHAPTER 8

Once Again, from the Top

Back at the studio that night, all the girls could think about was the experience at the homeless shelter.

"One lady told me that when her husband died, she lost their house and had nowhere to go," Anya shared. "I felt so bad."

"Me, too," Bria added. "I want to go back there and see Reese. She was just like us. She even dances."

Toni held up her hand. "Volunteering is wonderful, and I encourage you to do so. But there is a lot more we can do."

She pulled Bria to the center of the room.

"Since you seem to have the walk down, you are going to be the Little Tramp—and the rest of you are going to be society," she explained.

"What's society?" Gracie asked. "Is it like a club?"

"Sort of," Toni continued. "It's everyone else in the world. They don't understand what it means to be lonely, cold, hungry, and homeless. So they're going to turn their backs on Charlie. They're going to push him away." She demonstrated a graceful *pirouette* that landed her facing the back of the room. "You ignore him, shun him—no matter how hard he tries to make you laugh or get your attention."

"That sounds really mean," Anya said. "Why would we do that?"

"Because you are showing everyone in the audience how it feels to be homeless. When no one cares or hears you or understands what you are going through."

"Charlie has no voice," Bria said. "Like a silent movie."

"Exactly!" Toni said, patting her on the back.

"But we're going to give him one. At the end of the routine, I want you all to make a circle and lift him in the air. You're going to literally support him and accept him."

Liberty looked bored. "So, Bria gets to go up in the air and do a solo and everything and we get to dance around her? That doesn't sound fair."

Toni scowled. "Didn't you learn anything today at the shelter? Enough talking—all of you. I need to fix things."

Liberty sniffed and took her place in the back line. "If I was going to fix things, I'd make me the star and Bria the background dancer."

"Well, if I was going to fix things, I'd superglue your mouth shut," Rochelle tossed back.

"Ladies, I hear whispering," Miss Toni said, fumbling with the buttons on her MP3 player. "I want concentration. Not gabbing."

They ran the routine over and over again. Bria started by walking out onstage with the famous Chaplin waddle. She leaped through the air, then froze in an *attitude*, balancing on her right leg while holding her left at a 90-degree angle in front of her.

"Hold it, hold it," Toni coached her, "as if you're frozen in time. Now the rest of you . . . come forward. *Allongé!* Liberty, stretch out that *arabesque!*"

The girls swirled around her. "Let me see *balancé*—together! As one! Up, down, up, down, *relevé, fondu, relevé, fondu!*"

Bria started to wobble. Her leg was killing her from standing like a statue for thirty-two counts. "Now, Bria. Crouch down, get tiny, as if you're trying to hide from the world," Toni called. Grateful to drop her leg, Bria sunk to the floor and wrapped her arms around her knees.

Toni hit a button and the music came to an abrupt halt. Bria looked up, worried she'd done something wrong.

Toni pulled her up to her feet. "I'm not feelin' it," she said sternly.

Bria sighed. No matter how hard she tried, there was no pleasing her dance coach.

There was a knock at the studio. "May I make a suggestion?" J. J. said, poking his head inside.

Toni frowned. "Can you not eavesdrop?" She was pacing the floor, trying to come up with a way to make the routine work. Everyone was exhausted, physically and emotionally, from the entire day.

"Well, technically, it wasn't eavesdropping. It was more like eaveswatching. Through that teeny tiny crack in the door frame," J. J. said.

"The shades are drawn so no one can see in," Toni explained. "No one meaning you, too."

J. J. smiled and ignored her. "So I was thinking, why do we need any music?" he asked. "I mean, it's called 'Listen Up,' and it's about silent films. Wouldn't you get more attention if there was no sound at all—just motion?"

The girls looked at Toni for her reaction. "I can't tell what she's thinking," Scarlett whispered to Rochelle.

Toni cleared her voice. "I still hear whispering," she said. "And I have something important to say." She turned to face J. J. "I like his idea—but I think it needs tweaking."

J. J. raised an eyebrow. "Tweaking? What sort of tweaking? 'Cause people don't tweak Mr. J. J."

"I like the idea of no sound . . . until a point. Let's run it again," Toni commanded.

The Divas got back into position, and did the entire routine over, this time with no piano music. This time, when Bria crouched to the floor, Toni told her to cover her ears.

"Shut out the pain, the fear," she instructed her. "Give it eight counts, then open your arms wide! As if you're letting the rest of the world into *your* world."

"What do you hear?" J. J. asked.

Bria listened as hard as she could. "Um, Rochelle panting behind me? Liberty chewing her gum? Scarlett scratching her head?"

Toni gritted her teeth. "No. That's not what I want. Dismissed for tonight!"

Toni and J. J. huddled in the corner while the girls gathered up their bags.

"I was telling the truth," Bria said. "And I didn't even mention Anya grinding her teeth or Gracie licking her lips."

"I don't grind my teeth . . . do I?" Anya asked her teammates. "Maybe just when Toni barks."

Gracie licked her bottom lip. "I can't help it. I love this strawberry lip balm!"

"It doesn't matter," Scarlett said. "The point is we have less than two weeks before Electric Dance—and no routine or sound track." She glanced over at Miss Toni, who was deep in conversation with J. J. "I just hope they can figure something out by the time we get to Hollywood."

"If they don't, City Feet will trample all over us," Rochelle added.

Bria gulped. She couldn't think of anything worse.

CHAPTER 9

Hollywood, Here We Come!

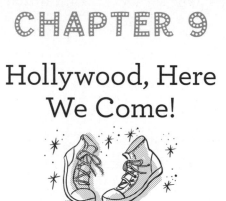

The flight to L.A. was five and a half hours, which was about five hours and twenty-nine minutes too long for Gracie.

"Are we there yet?" she asked, anxiously peering out the plane window.

"Not unless Hollywood is in the clouds," her mother answered. "Honey, relax. We'll be there before you know it."

Gracie sunk back in her seat. Why did the flight have to take forever? And why didn't Scarlett seem to mind? She was too busy reading some book about Old Hollywood.

"Did you know that one of Marilyn Monroe's favorite actors was Charlie Chaplin?" she read out loud.

"Cool. Maybe we could do a duet dressed like both of them," Bria suggested.

Rochelle looked back over her shoulder. Miss Toni was seated in the last row of the plane with J. J., studying her notebook of dance notations. "Somehow I don't think Toni would go for us changing up her choreography."

Bria shrugged. "I know. But it would be cool, don't ya think?"

"I think it would be cool if you would all stop talking. I'm trying to catch up on my beauty sleep." Liberty yawned.

Anya unfortunately had the seat next to her across the aisle. "The flight's only five hours. You need a lot more time than that," Anya muttered under her breath.

A voice came over the plane loudspeaker. "Ladies and gentlemen, we are making our final descent into LAX airport."

"Yippee!" Gracie squealed. "We're here!"

The girls gathered their luggage from the baggage carousel with Toni leading the way. "Okay, make sure you have everything. I don't want to get to Electric Dance missing any costumes or dance shoes."

Liberty had checked five bags—three filled with clothes, one brimming with hair products, and another containing enough makeup to stock a department store.

"And I thought I overpacked," Bria's mom whispered in her ear. "Compared to Liberty, I'm a lightweight!"

Just then, a voice came singing through the baggage claim area. "Darlings! Over here!" A blond woman dressed in a pink fur vest and huge black sunglasses made her way through the crowds.

Bria squinted. "Is that Lady Gaga?"

Rochelle sighed. "No, it's Mommy Montgomery."

"This way! This way!" Jane Montgomery instructed two limousine drivers wheeling luggage carts.

"Mommy!" Liberty screamed and raced toward her. *Mwah! Mwah!* They air-kissed on both cheeks. "I missed you so much!"

"And I missed my Libbylicious!" her mom said, hugging her.

"I think I'm going to barf," Rochelle groaned.

"Thanks for the warm welcome, Jane," Toni said as the drivers scooped up their bags. "And the ride."

"Of course! It's the least I can do for our dynamite Divas," she replied. "I hope you're all excited for your music video debut. I know the Sugar Dolls are excited to meet you."

"Wow! We get to meet them," Gracie gasped. "Yiphoo!" It was a funny word, but her combo of "yippee" and "yahoo" seemed to sum up what everyone was feeling.

Anya could barely contain her excitement. "I have always wanted to make a music video," she told Mrs. Montgomery. "I must have gone on a gazillion auditions when I lived out here. I can't believe it's really happening."

Jane nodded. "In Hollywood, it's all about who you know," she said, patting Anya on the head. "And you're lucky enough to know me."

J. J. stepped forward. "And you're lucky enough to know me. How's it goin', Janie?"

Jane's face went pale. She looked like she'd seen a ghost. "Jerome Fairbanks?" she gasped, taking off her sunglasses to get a better look. "What are you doing here? With my daughter's dance team?"

"He's our guest choreographer," Toni jumped in. "I hired him."

Jane stared. "You do know that he almost destroyed my career, right?"

"Hey, that was way back when," J. J. explained. "I was a pushy kid. A new dancer breaking into Hollywood."

"Pushy is right!" Jane continued to rant. "You practically *pushed* me off the stage when we were dancing backup for Madonna!"

"Technically, you were showin' off—I just put you back in your place." J. J. chuckled.

"Sound like someone else we know?" Rochelle whispered to her mom. "Liberty and Jane are two of a kind!"

"I won't allow him anywhere near my set—or my daughter," Jane insisted. "He's trouble."

"I may be trouble, but I won't give you any trouble," J. J. promised. "Scout's honor. Your daughter will vouch for me. Right, Liberty?"

Liberty squirmed. She knew better than to disagree with her mother, but she had to admit that J. J. was a pretty great choreographer. "Well, he did kind of move me to the front of the group routine . . ."

"So there you have it," Toni said. "There's nothing for you to worry about, Jane."

Liberty's mom didn't look convinced. "Fine. Just keep your distance!" she barked. "Everybody to the limo."

"Limo?" Bria asked. "Did she just say limo?"

"Is there any other way to ride?" Liberty replied.

"Uh, yeah . . . our usual team bus?" Rochelle said. "Remember? You're usually not that fancy."

"I know it's a bit over-the-top," Jane explained. "But it's Hollywood, darlings! I can't have our girls arriving in a bus to Electric Dance. Not when City Feet will be there trying to step all over everyone."

The Divas were so excited, they'd almost forgotten about City Feet!

"I can't wait to see the look on Mandy's face when we pull up in a limo," Liberty said. "I bet she cries."

"Eat your hearts out, Stinky Feet!" Gracie said, laughing.

Not even Rochelle could argue with that. Anything she could do to shake and rattle the competition was fine by her. "Let's pull right up to the hotel lobby," she suggested. "And honk the horn. We don't want them to miss our grand entrance."

Toni made a time-out sign with her hands. "You know how I feel about us mingling with the enemy," she warned them. "Don't look at them; don't talk to them."

"Just wave from the limo's sun roof!" Jane giggled. "Come on—let's go!"

Waiting for them in the parking lot was the hugest pink stretch limo the girls had ever seen. "It's a custom Range Rover that seats twenty," Jane boasted. "I borrowed it from Xtina."

"Christina Aguilera? Your mom knows Christina Aguilera?" Anya asked Liberty breathlessly.

"Oh yeah, like, forever," Liberty bragged. "I think she came to one of my birthday parties and sang that song from *Mulan*."

"Yes! It was your sixth birthday—a Disney Princesses party!" Jane recalled. "You were so precious as Cinderella. Remember the glass slippers I had Manolo make for you?"

"If I didn't barf before, I'm going to now," Rochelle moaned.

"No!" Bria said, squeezing her hand. "Not in the pretty pink limo. Don't ruin this for me! It's like a beautiful dream."

Everyone piled into the car, where Jane had cupcakes and pink lemonade waiting for them.

J. J. raised a glass. "To our humble host," he said, winking at Jane. "And to old friends."

Jane made a shocked face. "Do not think for one minute you are my friend," she said. "Beyoncé is my friend. Selena Gomez is my friend. But you? Never!"

Rochelle's mom tried to change the subject. "So tell us about this video. What will the girls be doing? They're so excited!"

Jane put down her lemonade glass and smiled. "Oh, it's divine. Literally. The song is called 'Heaven Sent' and they're going to be little angels walking on the clouds."

"What does my costume look like, Mommy?" Liberty asked. "I bet it's gorgeous."

"Of course!" Jane said, playfully tapping her on the tip of her nose. "It's silver sequins from top to bottom."

"The competition is tomorrow, and auditions for the video are on Friday," Toni reminded them. "I expect you all to be at your best for both." She pulled a third cupcake out of Gracie's hand. "That means eating healthy and getting lots of sleep before tomorrow."

"We'll be shooting all day Saturday and Sunday," Jane added. "And of course, one girl will be the lead angel." She looked over at Liberty and winked.

"So you'll be auditioning the girls for that lead part," J. J. added. "To keep things fair and square, right?"

"Yes, technically it's an open audition," Jane said, dismissing him with a wave of her hand. "The Sugar Dolls' manager insisted. But I make the final decision."

"So anyone can audition?" Anya asked. "There could be hundreds of girls there! Trust me, I went on a lot of open calls."

"They can audition all they want," Liberty said, licking pink vanilla frosting off the top of her cupcake. "But like my mother said, in Hollywood, it's who you know."

It didn't make Anya—or any of the Divas—feel much better. Even Toni looked disappointed. "I think we should concentrate on the competition," she said. "Once you all win first place in your divisions, we can talk about the audition and the video. Until then, I don't want to hear another word."

CHAPTER 10

The Agony of the Feet!

The limo pulled into the driveway of the hotel and honked its horn.

"We have arrived!" Jane announced. "Everyone out. Come meet your adoring fans."

She'd arranged to have a group of paparazzi greet them—not to mention "extra" actors begging for their autographs and chanting, "Divas! Divas!"

"What is this?" Toni said, stepping out of the limo and shielding her eyes from the popping camera flashes. "Where did these people come from?"

"It's called buzz, Toni." Jane took her aside. "It's how legends are born in Hollywood."

Toni looked like she was going to lose it. "This

is ridiculous. I don't need all this attention going to their heads." She pointed to Liberty and Gracie, who were blowing kisses to the crowd. "I need them to focus."

Out of the corner of her eye, Toni caught a glimpse of her archnemesis, Justine Chase. She and the rest of the City Feet had come outside to see what all the commotion was about.

"Oh, this is gonna be good!" Rochelle said, tugging Scarlett's arm. "Can't you see the steam coming out of Mean Justine's ears? She is really mad!"

"Nice entrance," Justine remarked. "Very subtle, Toni."

"It wasn't my idea." Toni nodded at Jane.

"Was it your idea to pay the actors to cheer for your team?" Justine continued. "So what's the going rate for fake fans?"

Mandy laughed. "That's so funny! The Divas have fake fans!"

Liberty stepped forward. "We couldn't even pay people to be your fans," she said. "There's not enough money in the world for it."

"Oh, nice one," Rochelle said, applauding Liberty. The girl really had a gift for zingers!

"We'll have tons of fans when we beat you," Phoebe told them. She struck a pose for the paparazzi. "Over here, guys. You should be taking pics of the real stars of Electric Dance!"

The photographers suddenly rushed at City Feet. Addison, Regan, Mandy, and Phoebe smiled and waved.

"Hey! Those are not your puppyrazzi!" Gracie protested.

"It's paparazzi," Scarlett corrected her. "And they can have them."

"Enough!" Miss Toni snapped. "Let's go inside and get to work."

CHAPTER 11

Ring around the Divas

Toni had booked a small extra room for the girls to run their routines, but Jane had other plans.

"I got you the Crystal Ballroom." She smiled. "It's much bigger and has such a wonderful ambiance."

Toni sighed. "The room I booked would have done just fine, Jane," she said. Then added through gritted teeth, "But thanks."

Rochelle was the first one up for practice. She still had no idea what she was wearing for her solo. Toni loved to keep her guessing.

"So, am I dancing in this?" she asked,

pointing to her red crop top and shorts. "Or you got something else for me?"

J. J. carried in a black wardrobe bag and unzipped it. "I thought this would do the trick." He pulled out a black leather jacket, black leggings, and a colorful graphic T-shirt—just like the outfit he'd worn the first day she met him. "Ya like?"

"It's so cool," she said, trying the jacket on for size. "It rocks."

"Then it's perfect," Toni said. "Now let's hope your dance is perfect as well."

Rochelle ran through the moves over and over, with J. J. shouting out the counts. When she was done, she collapsed on the floor waiting for Toni's feedback. Instead, there was silence.

"Well?" J. J. finally said. "Say something."

"Good," Toni replied. "It's good."

Rochelle sat up. "Good? Just good? It's awesome! It's crazy amazing! It's gonna knock those judges out of their seats!"

J. J. nodded. "Couldn't have said it better myself."

But Toni refused to elaborate further. "Let's just hope it's good enough to beat City Feet."

* * *

The Divas had never seen a dance competition quite like Electric Dance. The teams pulled out all the stops: there were lights, there were tricks, and there were over-the-top costumes.

"What is that supposed to be?" Bria asked as a giant white marshmallow suit made its way past her. Three boys trailed behind it, in beige jumpsuits, wearing backpacks.

"I could be wrong, but I think it's *Ghostbusters*," Rochelle said.

"Ooh, I love that movie!" Anya added. "*Who you gonna call? Ghostbusters!*"

Scarlett surveyed the backstage area. There were a lot of salutes to Hollywood—both old and new. She spotted a teen duet between "Scarlett O'Hara" and "Rhett Butler," a group dance to a *Harry Potter* theme, and a Shirley Temple Junior Solo.

"What's with the giant lollipop?" Rochelle asked her. "And all those curls?"

"'On the Good Ship Lollipop,'" Scarlett explained. "We have some serious competition here."

Toni looked just as concerned, especially when she saw Justine and City Feet take their places in the wings.

"What is *that?*" Liberty asked, noticing the stagehands decorating the ceiling with giant gold rings. The girls were each dressed in a simple gray cloak.

"*Lord of the Rings,*" Toni said, and sighed.

Liberty studied the drab costumes and made a face. "Don't they have any mirrors at Stinky Feet Studios?"

"You know Justine always has a trick up her sleeve," Scarlett said.

As the music thundered over the speakers, the girls burst onstage. Mandy reached up as a pair of gold rings floated down from the ceiling. She whipped off her cape to reveal a gold sequin leotard.

"She's going to do a gymnastics routine on the rings," Anya marveled. "Wow. This is like Cirque du Soleil!"

Gracie pushed through the Divas to get a better look. "I can do that," she said. "My gymnastics teacher taught me how."

"Now you tell us?" Liberty complained.

While Mandy twirled high above the stage, the rest of the girls de-cloaked to reveal gold-fringed skirts and halter tops. They raced around the stage doing an impressive acro routine of leaps, splits, and jumps. Regan and Addison performed a series of one-handed cartwheels while Phoebe showed off her *fouettés*.

"I lost count. How many turns was that?" Bria asked.

"A gazillion." Rochelle sighed. "They are really kicking our butts."

At the end of the dance, the judges gave them a standing ovation. The team strolled offstage past the Divas.

"Top that!" Addison boasted. "If we were in

the Olympics, that would have been a gold medal."

Rochelle elbowed Liberty. "You want to answer that one, or should I?"

"Be my guest," Liberty said, fuming. "I'm too disgusted."

Rochelle cleared her throat. "If you think your Lord of the Losers number is going to even come close to touching us, you're sadly mistaken."

"We'll see." Phoebe grinned. She looked at Bria's Charlie Chaplin costume. "Too bad that other team seems to have the same idea as you." She pointed to the wings where a group of boys were waiting to go on. They were dressed in black suits, hats, canes, and mustaches.

"Oh no!" Scarlett exclaimed. "It's the Little Tramp!"

"It's actually five of them." Bria gulped. "An army of Charlies!"

"Let's not panic." Scarlett tried to calm them down. "Our routine is really amazing."

"Performing a jazz routine called 'Funny You

Should Mention It,' please welcome the Oh Boy! Dance Studio from Omaha, Nebraska."

The five Chaplins lined up onstage and launched into a slapstick comedy jazz routine. One of them even sat on a judge's lap!

"Oh, this is just awful!" Bria cried.

"No, it's really good," Gracie said. "These guys are so funny!"

The number ended with one of the boys getting hit in the face with a whipped-cream pie.

Gracie burst out laughing. "I love them!"

Scarlett looked out at the audience, which was applauding wildly. "Yeah, the audience loves them, too. And you know Miss Toni always says that the judges like to see boy dance teams."

"I saw them and I don't like 'em," Rochelle said. "We're gonna look ridiculous following them with another Charlie Chaplin routine!"

Unfortunately, the Divas had no choice. The stagehands were already setting up their props, and the announcer called them to the wings.

"Dancing a contemporary routine called 'Listen

Up,' please put your hands together for the Dance Divas!"

It was so silent as Bria waddled out onstage that a pin drop could have been heard. She began to worry that having no music might have been a huge mistake. The audience looked confused.

"Go! Go!" J. J. whispered, pushing the rest of them out onstage. As Scarlett did her *grand jeté,* a strobe light pulsed above the stage. The effect made it look as if they were all in an old film from the 1920s. The sound of wind whistling came over the speakers, then cans being kicked and crows cawing. It was eerie and sad at the same time. Bria crouched down as the girls closed in around her. They tugged at her clothes and taunted her. Then, there was a single clap of thunder. Bria stretched her hands over her head and stood up. The Divas shed their black-and-white dresses to reveal rainbow-beaded leotards beneath them. The entire stage lit up in a kaleidoscope of colored lights. Anya and Liberty lifted Bria up and hoisted her onto Scarlett's and Rochelle's shoulders.

Gracie pulled a red rose from behind her back and handed it to her. Their fingers touched as Bria took the rose and sniffed it. The words DIGNITY, COMPASSION, and LOVE flashed behind them with images of the Divas working at the soup kitchen. Then the entire stage went pitch-black except for a single spotlight shining on the rose in Bria's outstretched hand.

When the lights came on for their bows, the audience was already on its feet cheering. Miss Toni looked pleased.

J. J. greeted them backstage. "You girls kicked it!" he said. "That was cray-zee to the tenth degree!"

Bria peeled the mustache off her lip. "It was pretty good, huh?" she said breathlessly.

"It was so good that there's no sign of those Feet anywhere," Rochelle said, looking around for their rivals.

"We must have scared off those Lord of the Ring-Dings!" Liberty added.

But if there was one thing the Divas had

learned in the past, it was to never underestimate their rivals. The announcer had already called for the solo and duet competitors to line up backstage. Yet there was no sign of City Feet and their coach.

"I have a bad feeling about this," Bria whispered to Scarlett. "A really, really bad feeling."

CHAPTER 12

You Gotta Have Heart

Toni ducked backstage to congratulate the girls on their performance. "I saw a few glitches, but overall, great job," she said. "I think it had a very strong message about helping the homeless, and the judges seemed very moved."

J. J. agreed. "If that doesn't win first place, I'll eat Bria's hat," he said, taking her black bowler and placing it on his head.

"Then I hope you're hungry," said a voice behind him. It was Justine.

"Your little statement about the plight of the homeless was very touching," she addressed Toni. "It broke my heart."

"I didn't know you had one," Toni fired back. "Nice to know."

Justine didn't seem at all fazed. "Cute, Toni. Very cute. But you should really put your money where your mouth is."

"Meaning?" Toni asked.

"Meaning I just had a lovely chat with the judges. City Feet had a group meeting and unanimously voted to donate any and all of its winnings today to the St. Ignatius Homeless Shelter."

"Hold up! That's our homeless shelter!" Rochelle protested.

"Is it? That's so interesting!" Justine added. "Because when I called them just now, they said you hadn't promised them any of your prize winnings. They were so happy to hear from us, and so touched with our generosity."

"We spent hours working there!" Bria said. "You haven't done anything for those people."

"Well, we are doing something now." Justine smiled. "And I can't tell you how impressed the

Electric Dance judges are. I do believe it earned us some serious brownie points."

"You can't do that!" Bria exclaimed.

"No, Bria, they can and they should," Toni corrected her. "I wish we had thought of it first. I'm not going to stop City Feet from giving much-needed money to St. Ignatius."

"I'm so glad." Justine smiled. "But just so we're clear, you couldn't stop us even if you tried."

"You always did like taking credit for other people's ideas," Toni said, tossing back, "I haven't forgotten about Spring Recital."

Bria looked confused. "What's she talking about?" she whispered to Scarlett.

"Beats me," Scarlett replied. "Toni and Justine have a lot of history."

"Oh puh-lease!" Justine waved her hand in the air, dismissing Toni's comment. "Are you still holding a grudge for that silly little mistake on the ABC program?"

"Silly mistake? You told them to print that

you choreographed the entire ballet—when it was my senior project!" Toni shouted.

"Are we talking about something that happened in high school?" J. J. stepped between the two dance coaches to referee. "Ladies, that is water under the bridge."

"You had no right trying to gain favor with the judges for my team's hard work," Toni insisted. It was a good thing J. J. was in her way. She wanted to wipe that smile off of Justine's face!

Justine batted her eyelashes. "Toni, haven't you figured it out yet? I am always one step ahead of you." She skipped back to the audience.

"Wow. Did anyone else feel a chill when she walked by?" J. J. said. "I wondered why everyone calls her Mean Justine. Now I know."

"It's so not fair!" Bria protested.

"Like you're surprised?" Liberty said. "Does City Feet *ever* play fairly?"

"We've done all we can," Toni said. "Right now, we just need to focus on the rest of the competition. They haven't won yet—so let's not jump to conclusions." She and J. J. went off to run through the cues and props for the next routines with the stagehands.

Bria shook her head. "But we're the ones who did the whole number about the homeless. We're the ones who volunteered. They couldn't care less. They're only donating the money to impress the judges."

"Maybe the judges will see through their pitiful attempt to one-up us," Scarlett suggested.

"There has to be something else we could do," Bria said.

"We could tell the judges we'll donate our winnings, too," Anya suggested.

A lightbulb went off over Bria's head. "Or we could donate even more money than City Feet promised and *really* make a difference for the shelter."

Rochelle looked puzzled. "Hey, Bri, did you win the lottery and forget to tell us? We don't have any money."

Bria searched the audience for the person she

was looking for, the one person she knew who had the connections to pull off a scheme even sneakier than Justine's. She spied Jane Montgomery in the back of the audience, texting away on her cell phone.

"Come with me," she said grabbing Liberty by the hand. "I think I know how to fix this!"

CHAPTER 13

In Sync

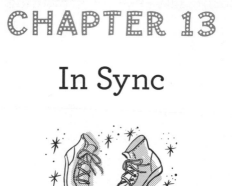

There was no time to wonder what Bria and Liberty were up to. Scarlett and Rochelle had to go head-to-head against Phoebe in the Junior Solo category.

"What is she supposed to be?" Rochelle asked, peering out onstage. Phoebe was wearing a black tuxedo jacket and adjusting the cuff links at her wrists.

"She's Bond, James Bond," Anya said, reading the program.

"She's boring, SO BORING!" Rochelle added, watching Phoebe's contemporary routine. "I'm falling asleep."

"Yeah, it's just missing something," Scarlett agreed.

Phoebe's steps were sleek and technically perfect with an amazing *battement* combination in the middle. Yet it lacked energy, enthusiasm, and excitement: Miss Toni's "3E's" for winning.

Anya checked the program. "You guys are up next," she told Rochelle and Scarlett.

Scarlett made sure her blond wig was pinned tightly in place and her red lipstick wasn't smudged. She didn't need a fashion faux pas.

"You can do it," Rochelle said, hugging her friend. "Don't forget to do *the face*."

Scarlett took the center of the stage in her pointe shoes. She tried to remember everything Toni had told her: be strong yet fragile, graceful yet sad. She reminded herself to think of the moment her parents told her they were divorcing. She felt her eyes sting.

"Wow, she is so into it," Anya whispered in the wings.

"She does good tippy-toes," Gracie added, referring to Scarlett's *bourrées* across the stage.

Scarlett finished with a *grand jeté* that looked as if she was flying through the air. The audience applauded wildly as she kneeled, stretched her arms out to the judges, and raised her eyes upward. The spotlight got smaller until it only focused on her face. Scarlett could feel the tears spilling down her cheeks.

"You were awesome!" Rochelle said, catching her bestie as she ran backstage.

"Really? I was so swept up in the emotion, I think I was a little wobbly on the *pirouettes*," Scarlett replied.

"You were the embodiment of Marilyn," said a voice behind her. Toni swooped in to congratulate her. "That was an emotional tour de force. The judges were passing around the tissue box."

"And now it's your turn," J. J. told Rochelle. "Do me proud, Rock."

Rochelle nodded. She felt the butterflies flutter in the pit of her stomach and her heart began to pound. She held on to that nervous energy and used it to explode onto the stage with a handspring.

"Whoa!" Gracie gasped. "That was cool!"

"She's fierce," J. J. said, grinning. His prized pupil had the audience on their feet, clapping to the beat as she rocked it out. She kicked her feet straight in front of her, then shuffled left and right before executing a perfect back walkover.

"Was that the Cupid Shuffle?" Scarlett asked.

"I prefer the J. J. Shuffle," the choreographer replied. "I gave it my own twist." Rochelle suddenly jumped up on the toes of her sneakers and spun in a circle.

The judges jumped out of their seats and clapped enthusiastically.

"Well, whaddaya know, a standing O!" J. J. exclaimed. "Not bad, eh, Toni?"

Toni kept a perfectly straight face. "I'll let you know when I see their scores."

Rochelle raced back to the wings, still pumped from the routine.

"That was the best I have ever danced!" she told her teachers and teammates.

"Really? Because I saw sloppy feet and bent legs all over the place," Toni corrected her. "It was exuberant, but far from technically perfect."

Rochelle looked at J. J., hoping for a better review. "What did you think?"

"I think the Rochelle Shuffle may be the hot new dance," he said, winking. "I saw those judges shaking their booties."

Rochelle sighed. At least *someone* approved.

"Don't take it personally," Scarlett whispered. "Toni's just distracted and upset over the whole St. Ignatius thing."

Bria and Liberty reappeared. "I think we have a solution," Bria said. She pointed to the stage, where Mrs. Montgomery was having a few words with the announcer.

"Oh no. Bri, what did you do?" Scarlett asked nervously.

"Ladies and gentlemen," the announcer bellowed into the mike. "May I have your attention please? It seems we have some VIPs in the audience who would like to come up here and say a few words."

"VIPs? What is he talking about?" Rochelle asked.

The announcer cleared his throat and held his hand in the air to silence the buzz in the audience. "Please, put your hands together for THE SUGAR DOLLS!"

CHAPTER 14

All Dolled Up

The room suddenly exploded with screams, cheers, and chants as the pop stars made their way onstage. Even City Feet couldn't contain their excitement.

"OMG! I love them!" Mandy squealed and raced to the wings to get a closer look. "Baby Doll is my favorite. She is so cute!"

"I love Rag Doll!" Addison added. "Her clothes are the coolest!"

"What are they doing here?" Scarlett asked Bria and Liberty.

"Let's just say, they did us a huge favor."

Liberty smiled. "They were just down the block at their recording studio, and they were more than happy to come and announce their big fundraiser."

Toni raised an eyebrow. "What fundraiser?"

Bria was happy when the Dolls interrupted Miss Toni's question and she didn't have to answer her. She wasn't sure how she'd feel about her going to Liberty's mom and asking for help without letting her know beforehand. But the way Bria saw it, there wasn't any other choice.

"Hey, dolls!" Candy Doll said, taking the microphone. She tossed lollipops from her purse into the crowd. "We're so excited to be here!"

"Totally!" Baby Doll chimed in. She wore a pacifier necklace and carried a pink blankie. "We wanted to share with you something really cool that we're going to be doing with our next video."

Toni glanced at Bria, who could tell her teacher didn't like the sound of this.

"We're really excited to hear that one of the dance groups here has been doing amazing things to help the homeless," Sporty Doll continued.

"That's us! That's us!" Mandy jumped up and down. "They heard we're donating our money to the homeless!"

"Miss Toni, would you mind coming up here?" Jazzy Doll requested.

Mandy's jaw dropped. "No way! They have the wrong team!"

"*Shhh!*" Addison elbowed her. "Would you be quiet, Mandy? Justine stole the idea from their dance number anyway."

"Yoo-hoo! Miss Toni!" Rag Doll called. "Where are you?"

Toni's cheeks flushed red. "Go on." J. J. gave her a little shove. "The whole St. Ignatius thing was your idea. Tell 'em."

Toni took the stage and shook hands with each of the Dolls.

"She's gonna kill us," Anya said, watching her teacher squirm. "Bri, what were you thinking?"

"I was thinking that we deserve the credit,"

Bria replied. "It was Miss Toni who had her heart in the right place, not Justine."

Toni cleared her throat. "Thank you," she said simply. "I'm glad I have the opportunity to tell you what my Divas and I have been doing at St. Ignatius Homeless Shelter. We've been volunteering at the soup kitchen, preparing meals and handing them out to the homeless families. We've sat with them, talked to them, and pitched in however we could. It's been a life-changing experience for all of us."

J. J. waved from the wings and gave her a thumbs-up. "You go, girl!" he shouted.

"It's truly been our privilege to do this," Toni continued. "We've been very moved by what's going on in our very own community, and we intend to continue helping in any way we can."

Rag Doll spoke up. "We'd like to help you help them," she said. "So we're donating part of the proceeds of our new video, 'Heaven Sent,' to St. Ignatius. Every time someone downloads the song and video, the shelter will be getting money."

Toni's eyes grew wide. "That could be millions of dollars."

"Let's hope!" Baby Doll said. "Good job, Divas! Let's hear it for them!" The crowd began chanting "Divas! Divas!"

"I think we just one-upped Justine's one-up," Rochelle said. She glanced over to see the City Feet coach pouting in the corner and Mandy throwing a tantrum.

"The important thing is that we are going to make a lot of money for St. Ignatius," Bria pointed out. "That's what matters."

"It is what matters," Toni said, returning to her team backstage. "But you know how I feel about sneaking around and not playing fair, Bria."

"Aw, come on," J. J. said. "Those Feet didn't play fair. Bria was just evening the field."

"I'm sorry," Bria said. "I wanted to help."

"It's very generous of the Dolls to do this," Toni said. "And I'm sure the shelter will be thrilled. But I won't have any of you stooping to

Justine's level. Is that clear? Next time, Bria, you come to me instead of going behind my back. Clear?"

Bria nodded. "Yes, Miss Toni."

"I think it's awesome," J. J. spoke up. "That money is going to make a huge difference in so many lives. I wish I had thought of it."

Liberty interjected, "Excuse me? I convinced my mom this would be great publicity for the Sugar Dolls," Liberty interjected. "Isn't someone going to thank me?"

"If you get out there and do a flawless duet, I'll thank you," Toni said to Liberty and Bria. "If you mess it up, not even the Sugar Dolls can save you."

CHAPTER 15

Yee-Haw Cowgirls

It took the announcer several minutes to calm the crowd down after the Sugar Dolls' appearance. "Yes, that was very exciting, wasn't it?" he said, trying to be heard over the cheers. "And here's something else that's exciting: our next category, Junior Duets. Please put your hands together for our first pair, Bria and Liberty from Dance Divas Studio doing an acro routine to 'Lone Ranger Rewind.'"

The girls galloped onstage and took their positions. Liberty and Bria were dressed in black catsuits, cowboy hats, and silver vests. "Hi-ho, Silver!

Away!" they shouted as they launched into an amazing series of splits and tumbles.

"Nice needle," Anya said, watching Liberty stretch her leg straight behind her and touch her head to her knee.

"I think Bria's better," Rochelle insisted. "Did you see that back walkover from her sitting position?"

"They're both amazing," Scarlett said. "They have to win. They just have to!"

At the end of the number, they pushed two mechanical "horses" into the middle of the stage and climbed into the saddle.

"Let's pray this works," Anya said, crossing her fingers.

The saddles bumped up and down, backward and forward, as the girls held on to the reins.

Liberty took off her cowboy hat and waved it in the air. But Bria didn't look as comfortable and confident in the saddle.

"What's up with Bria?" Rochelle asked Scarlett. "She looks green."

"Oh no," Scarlett replied. "It's the Tilt-A-Whirl all over again."

The audience cheered as the saddles rocked back and forth, faster and faster. Bria held her breath and hoped that she wouldn't barf right there on the stage. When the horses finally stopped moving, they climbed off. Liberty took her bow, but Bria raced offstage, straight for the bathroom.

"Outta my way!" she cried, pushing past City Feet and her own teammates.

"What's the matter, Bria?" Phoebe called after her. "Did you get a little sick from your dance? I did, too."

"Lay off, Phoebe," Liberty warned her. She had her cowboy hat back on her head and looked like she meant business. "I'm sure your routine with Addison is going to make us all lose our lunches."

"I don't know about your lunches," Addison retaliated. "But you'll definitely lose the first prize trophy. Watch and weep." She and Phoebe peeled off their hoodies to reveal rhinestone-studded leotards and blond wigs.

"I told Toni I wanted to wear rhinestones," Liberty bristled. "Those costumes are so much better than ours!"

"Seriously? Are they Marilyn?" Rochelle gasped. "Scarlett, they stole your character."

Scarlett shrugged. First there were too many Charlies and now there were multiple Marilyns. No matter what the Divas did, they couldn't catch a break.

"Let's give a warm welcome to Phoebe and Addison from City Feet Dance Studio dancing a jazz routine to 'Diamonds Are a Girl's Best Friend'!" the announcer said into the microphone. A crystal chandelier descended from the ceiling and twinkled in the spotlight. The girls did multiple kicks, flicks, and leaps. The music switched from Marilyn singing to an electrifying version of Madonna's "Material Girl." They were on fire!

"Oh no," Anya cried. "It gets worse by the minute. They are killing us!"

Bria made her way back to the wings, leaning on her mom, and sat down on the floor. "You okay, Bri?" Scarlett asked her. "Can we get you some water? A cold washcloth?"

"A barf bag?" Liberty said, smirking.

Bria shook her head. "No, I'm okay. I felt much better when I splashed some water on my face."

"Too much Tilt-A-Horse?" Scarlett tried to cheer her up.

"I guess," Bria said, smiling weakly. "At least I didn't throw up onstage. That would have lost us the Junior Duet title for sure."

"Take a look out there." Liberty motioned to the stage. "We've already lost it." Phoebe and Addison were doing *arabesques* in perfect sync.

"Their technique is sick," Anya said, sighing.

"Please," Bria begged. "Don't say sick."

The audience and the judges gave them a standing ovation.

"I guess horses aren't a girl's best friend," Addison said as she shoved past Liberty in the hallway. She sniffed in the air. "Do you smell something, Pheebs?"

Phoebe wrinkled her nose. "Yeah, it smells like a stable. Oh, wait!" She got in Liberty's face. "That must be you!"

"Liberty," Scarlett warned, holding her teammate back. "It's not worth it. Remember what Miss Toni said about sinking to their level."

"All I was going to say is 'Good luck!'" Liberty replied with a forced smile. "You'll need it."

It took the judges two hours to deliberate and compile their list of winners.

"Do you think we stand a chance?" Bria asked Scarlett.

Scarlett peeked out at the judges' table. "Who knows? We all did the best we could."

The Divas sat onstage, trying not to look nervous. "Don't let them see you sweat," Rochelle whispered to Gracie. "Calm, cool, and collected. That's us."

Gracie nodded. "I'm cool as a pickle," she said.

"I think you mean cool as a cucumber," Anya corrected her.

"No, I mean pickle. I like pickles. Especially supersour ones."

"Gracie, if we win first prize in the Junior Group dance, I will buy you a whole jar of pickles," Scarlett assured her.

"Thanks, Scoot!" Gracie said, smiling.

The Divas had to sit through several awards until they announced the Junior Solo category. "In third place, 'On the Good Ship Lollipop,' Hashtag Dance Studios, Los Angeles," the announcer read.

"Local favorite," Anya said. "The judges love them."

"And in second place . . . 'Breakable,' Scarlett Borden from Dance Divas Studio, Scotch Plains, New Jersey!"

Scarlett leaped up to accept her trophy. She caught her teacher glaring at her from the audience. She knew second place wasn't good enough for Toni.

"Finally, our first place Junior Solo award goes to 'Rising Star,' Rochelle Hayes from Dance Divas again!"

"Rock! That's you!" Bria squealed.

"It's me!" Rochelle exclaimed, jumping to her feet. J. J. was standing on his chair in the ballroom, pumping his fists in the air.

Scarlett hugged her BFF. "If someone had to beat me, I'm glad it was you!" she said. "You deserved it, Rock! Congrats!"

The trios and duets were the next to be announced. The *Ghostbusters* trio took home first place and the *Gone with the Wind* duet earned third place. It was down to Divas and City Feet for the top two spots in duets.

Bria covered her ears. "I can't listen," she said. "I just can't."

The announcer tapped the mike to make sure it was on. "Okay, this one was a close one. Just one-tenth of a point separates our first- and second-place winners," he began. "In first place: 'Diamonds Are a Girl's Best Friend,' Phoebe

Malone and Addison Gates from City Feet Dance Studio, Long Island!"

Bria's heart sank. Her queasiness had cost them the trophy. "I'm really sorry, Liberty," she told her partner.

"Why are *you* sorry?" Liberty replied. "You held on to those reins and didn't let go, even though you were ready to barf. That's pretty impressive."

"Really?" Bria said. "You're not mad at me?"

"Mad at you? No. Mad at those Stinky Feet? Yes. You better believe it. But the best Junior Group hasn't been announced yet."

Toni and J. J. made their way to the front row. They wanted to be up close for the final awards.

"Great. She's closing in so she can kill us when we lose," Rochelle said.

The other Charlie Chaplin routine came in fourth. "Oh great," Anya groaned. "The judges don't like Charlies. We're doomed."

Bria glanced over at City Feet. Surprisingly, they all looked just as petrified.

"In second place," the announcer paused. The Divas all held their breath. " 'Listen Up,' Dance Divas Studio, New Jersey!"

The girls all looked at each other. No one even wanted to go up and take the trophy. "You go get it, Gracie," Scarlett said, elbowing her little sister. Gracie raced up and grabbed the trophy out of the announcer's hands and held it above her head.

"I'm glad someone's happy," Liberty said grumpily.

"Finally, our first place Junior Group winners, *Lord of the Rings,*' City Feet, Long Island!"

Justine and her team descended upon the announcer and blew kisses to the audience. "We just want to say we're giving all of our winnings to that homeless shelter!" Mandy yelled into the mike.

"Ugh, she doesn't even know its name!" Bria complained. "This is so unfair. After all we did with the Sugar Dolls, the judges still picked them."

"That's right. They did." Miss Toni appeared behind them onstage. "And do you know why? Because their routine was better than ours. Not because they promised to give money to the homeless shelter or because we called in a VIP favor. Because they deserved it, plain and simple."

"It doesn't make it hurt any less," Bria said.

"No, it doesn't. Losing always hurts. But there will be another competition, and another chance to beat City Feet," Toni replied. "I'm proud of you girls."

Rochelle raised an eyebrow. "You are? Even though we blew it?"

"You did a lot more than dance these past two weeks. You made a difference in people's lives. That's the biggest win in my book."

"Mine, too," J. J. said. "Plus, my choreography brought us a first prize trophy . . . Just sayin'."

"Your choreography and these talented toes," Rochelle reminded him.

"I hate it when we get beat," Gracie said,

eyeing Mandy, who was sticking her tongue out in their direction.

"There's always tomorrow," Miss Toni said. "And for us, tomorrow is a big day."

"Oh my gosh! I almost forgot about the Sugar Dolls' video!" Bria exclaimed.

"I didn't forget," Liberty said. "And my audition is going to be unforgettable!"

CHAPTER 16

Lights, Camera, Divas!

When the team arrived at 7:00 a.m. at the Hollywood studio for the Dolls' video shooting, they couldn't believe their eyes. The green room was filled with girls of all ages who wanted to be backup dancers in their video. The only ones missing were City Feet, who already flew home to celebrate winning first.

"I told you," Anya said. "I've been on open calls before. There could be thousands of girls auditioning."

Liberty spied her mother, talking to one of the Dolls' managers in the back of the room. "Mommy! Mommy!" she shouted. "We're here!"

Jane Montgomery waved but continued making notes on her clipboard.

"What's the matter, Libbylicious?" Rochelle whispered in her ear. "Mommy too busy for you?"

This time, it was Toni who stepped in to referee. "Instead of insulting each other, why don't you go stretch and warm up," she commanded. "I'm going to see where we are in the lineup."

Their teacher passed through the crowds of girls and coaches and made her way over to Jane. "Quite a turnout," she said. "When are the Divas up?"

The Sugar Dolls' manager was a tall man with spiky red hair and sunglasses. He looked down at Toni over the tip of his nose. "Take a number," he said dismissively.

"Sorry," she said to Toni. "Busy, busy! It might be a little wait, but I'll make sure the girls get to show their stuff." She followed the manager out of the room.

Toni walked back to her team. "Well?" Liberty asked. "Do we get to go in now?"

Toni held up the number 128 written in red on a slip of paper. "This is our number," she said. "There are one hundred twenty-seven other dancers in front of you."

"We'll be here all day!" Gracie whined. "I'm tired. And hungry."

"Welcome to the world of showbiz," J. J. said, handing Gracie a granola bar. "It's a lot of waiting around."

"Which means you all need to have patience," Toni said. "I don't need to remind you that anywhere you go, you are representing my studio. I expect you all to behave accordingly."

* * *

It was nearly two hours before Jane returned to the green room with her clipboard to start calling girls in for the auditions. "Numbers one through fifteen, please report to the stage," she said.

"Fifteen? They're only up to fifteen?" Bria exclaimed. "Liberty, that's your mom up there. Go do something!"

Liberty tried to motion to her mom over the packed room, but it was no use. "She's in work mode," she said, and sighed. "It's like talking to a brick wall when she's in the zone."

"Uh-huh," J. J. said, piping up. "I am very familiar with that zone." Then he got an idea. "Sometimes your mom just needs a little wake-up call. Get your dance shoes and come with me. But don't tell Toni—she'll freak."

The Divas did as they were told and followed J. J. through a back door to the soundstage where the Dolls were holding their auditions.

"Oh my gooshness! There they are!" Gracie squealed.

Scarlett clamped her hand over her little sister's mouth. "Gracie, keep quiet! Do you want to ruin the plan?" she asked.

"What's the plan?" Anya asked her.

"I'm not sure. But J. J. knows what he's doing. I think."

Scarlett looked around, but their choreographer had disappeared.

"He told us to stay put," Bria said. "And to prepare to be dazzled . . . whatever that means."

The Sugar Dolls' "Heaven Sent" song boomed over the speakers as Jane struggled to teach the first group of dancers the choreography. "And a five-six-seven-eight . . . ," she shouted, demonstrating a series of kicks, turns, and jumps.

"Move over, Janie!" A voice suddenly rang through the soundstage. "Lemme show you how it's done!"

J. J. burst onto the stage. He launched into a breakdancing routine, spinning on his head.

"Stop that this minute, Jerome! Do you hear me?" Jane was bright red in the face and looked like she was going to explode. J. J. did several flips and twirls before landing on his feet right in front of Jane.

"I do believe I have upstaged you once again," he said, and chuckled.

All the girls onstage applauded.

"Get out!" Jane screeched. "This is my video!"

"Whose video is it?" asked a female voice in

the audience. It was Toni, and she was sitting with the Sugar Dolls watching everything. "I believe it's the Sugar Dolls' video," Toni corrected. "And we've just been discussing how they are open to some collaboration."

"What's a cola-bration?" Gracie asked, scratching her head. "Is that like a party with soda?"

"Better," Scarlett said. "It means Miss Toni has a plan!"

Toni walked up to the stage with the Dolls at her side. "It seems that the Sugar Dolls believe that in art and videos, authenticity is everything." She winked at J. J.

"Meaning?" Jane asked.

"Meaning that we'd like to shoot the finale for 'Heaven Sent' in New Jersey at the St. Ignatius Homeless Shelter," Rag Doll spoke up. "Toni tells us it's an amazing place and the inside of a church would be a great spot for the big dance finale of 'Heaven Sent.'"

"Yes!" shouted a voice from the wings. It was Bria, and she couldn't contain her excitement. "That is so amazing!"

Both Jane and Liberty gave her a dirty look, but Baby Doll walked over and took her hand. "And since it was all your idea to get us involved with St. Ignatius, I think it's only fair that your friends be our backup dancers and you be our spotlight dancer."

"What?" screamed Liberty. "No way!"

"OMG! Me? Really?" Bria gasped.

"Absolutely not." Jane shook her head. "We have all these girls still left to audition."

"That's too bad," Toni said. "Because we all have a flight to make if we want to shoot at St. Ignatius tomorrow bright and early. I called and cleared it with the church staff."

"Awesome!" said Sporty Doll. "This will be the coolest video we've ever made."

"I haven't even finalized the choreography," Jane protested. "Or scouted the location, or approved the costumes, the lighting, the sound . . ."

J. J. put his arm around Jane. "You know. That's always been your problem," he said. "Too much planning. Sometimes, you gotta roll with it."

Jane pushed his arm off her shoulder. "Jane Montgomery does *not* roll with it."

"But the Divas do!" Bria piped up.

"And the Dolls do!" added Baby Doll.

"Then ladies," Toni said, smiling, "I believe we have a plane to catch."

CHAPTER 17

Dance Divas and Dolls

Bria was jet-lagged from the long flight back home, but she wasn't about to let it stand in her way. She stifled a yawn as she made her way down the stairs of her house, careful not to wake up her dad and sister, who were still fast asleep.

"Have some breakfast," her mom said, placing a plate of scrambled eggs and toast on the kitchen table. It was 5:00 Saturday morning, and Mrs. Chang had already been up for an hour cooking and packing everything they needed for the video shoot.

"Mom, you're too much!" Bria said, digging

into her plate. "I know sometimes I tell you that you're too tough on me, but—"

"Sometimes? How about all the time?" her mother interjected.

"Okay, *all* the time. But I really appreciate everything you do for me."

Her mom stopped sipping her cup of coffee and smiled. "I do it because I love you, Bri. And I know you have it in you to do great things. I believe in you."

"You do?" Bria asked.

"Of course I do! And Miss Toni and all those Sugar Babies believe in you, too."

"Sugar *Dolls*," Bria said, giggling.

"Oh, whatever you call them," her mom replied. "And I'm very proud that you're doing this for a great cause. You know what I want you to be when you grow up?"

Bria wrinkled her nose. "A journalist like Dad? President of the United States? The first woman on Mars?"

"All of the above sounds fine," she replied, laughing. "But most of all, I want you to be a good person with a big heart who tries to make the world a better place." She put her arms around Bria and hugged her tight. "And you've already proved to me that you are."

✳ ✳ ✳

St. Ignatius was bustling with activity: cameras and lights were going up, and even a huge "cloud" backdrop was being rolled up a huge ramp mounted on the front steps of the church. Jane Montgomery stood in the middle of all the mayhem, barking orders.

"Careful with those costumes—they cost me a fortune!" she called as a location truck unloaded garment bags on racks.

Bria and her mom pulled into the parking lot. "Wow," Bria said, climbing out of the car. "This is crazy." A man pushed past her carrying a glittering harp.

Inside, the other Divas, their moms, and J. J. were gathered and waiting for wardrobe, hair, and makeup.

"Hi, guys!" Bria called.

"Make way for the star of the show!" J. J. said teasingly.

Liberty silently pouted. She hated when anyone else stole the spotlight.

"Where's Miss Toni?" Bria asked.

Scarlett shrugged. "Don't know. We saw her a few minutes ago and then she disappeared."

Bria looked around the shelter, hoping to spot Reese. She knew how excited she would be that the Sugar Dolls were filming there.

"Excuse me," she asked one of the shelter's staff. "Have you seen a girl named Reese and her mom, Jenny? I talked to them last time I was here."

The woman checked a list of names on a clipboard. "I'm sorry, dear," she replied. "I don't see anyone by that name here. Do you know her last name?"

Bria wanted to kick herself: Why hadn't she thought to ask? "I'm sorry I don't." All she had was her e-mail address.

"Well, maybe she'll come later. People drop in

all day and night. The door is always open," the woman said.

Mrs. Chang saw how disappointed Bria looked. "What's wrong, honey? I thought you'd be so excited to be shooting your first big music video."

"I am," Bria said. "I'm just missing somebody, that's all." She sent Reese an e-mail on her laptop and hoped she'd get it in time to meet the Sugar Dolls:

Hi, Reese, it's Bria. At St. I's! URGENT!

But there was no reply.

Jane ran through how the entire choreography would go. The Dolls would dance through the rows of pews in the church while the Divas twirled around behind them, dressed like their mini-mes. The costumes were breathtaking: gold sequin dresses topped with silver leather jackets and cool knee-high leather boots.

"Oh my gooshness! I feel like a pop star!" Gracie said, twirling in her outfit. She was Baby

Doll's mini-me and wore a rhinestone-studded pacifier around her neck.

Liberty held up a gold-and-white swirled lollipop. "The least they could have done was made me Rag Doll," she said, and sighed. "I love her clothes!"

"I don't know what you're complaining about," Rochelle said as Sporty Doll. "I've gotta dance while swinging this!" She held up a gold tennis racquet.

"I wish Reese could be here to see this," Bria said. "She would be in heaven!"

She sent her another e-mail:

Where R U? Come to St. Ignatius ASAP.

I have a huge surprise!

She waited patiently and refreshed her e-mail. But there was still no reply.

"Maybe she's busy studying?" Scarlett suggested.

"Or maybe she's ignoring me because she doesn't want to be my friend," Bri answered.

Jane clapped her hands. "I need my backup dancers in position now! Divas, that's you!"

Suddenly, Bria spotted a familiar face at the entrance to the church, trying to get past the Dolls' bodyguards. Reese! She raced over and pleaded with the big, muscly security men to let her friend in.

"Bria!" Reese waved at her. "I was at the library when I got your e-mail!"

But the guards stood tall. Bria raced over. "Please, let her in. She's with me!"

"Sorry, we have our orders," one of the guards replied. "Only talent on set."

"But she is talent!" Bria said. She remembered Reese's amazing dancing. She thought quickly: "She's one of the Divas."

"I am?" Reese asked, surprised. "I mean, I am! Totally!"

The guard stepped aside and Bria grabbed Reese's arm. "I'm so glad you're here!" she said.

"I got here as fast as I could," Reese said. She gazed around the room. "This is amazing! I can't believe I'm so close to the Sugar Dolls!"

Bria smiled. "Come with me. I think I know a way you can get a lot closer!"

CHAPTER 18

Guess Who?

It took another two hours for all the props, lights, and cameras to get into position, but finally, they were ready to shoot.

"This better be good, Jane. We're expecting you to deliver like you said you would," the Sugar Dolls' manager said.

Jane rubbed her temples. "When I say *action* I want to see the Dolls sweep in. Divas, hold your places till I give you the cue."

The music for "Heaven Sent" filled the entire church. "*A little bit of love, a little bit of kindness, the time we spent was Heaven Sent . . .*" The Dolls lip-synched the lyrics as they danced.

"Now, cue Divas!" Jane shouted. There, dressed like the Sugar Dolls, were Scarlett, Gracie, Rochelle, Liberty, Anya . . . and Reese!

"Wait! Cut! Why are there six of you? I choreographed a routine for five Dolls and five backup dancers. Who's this?" She pointed to Reese.

"I'm sorry," Reese apologized. "I just wanted to be in the video and meet the Dolls."

Jane was starting to pull her hair out. "This is what I get for working with amateurs! Security! Throw this imposter out!"

"No, wait! It's all my fault," Bria spoke up. "I told Reese it was okay. I found an extra costume and pinned it on her."

"That's okay, Bria. You tried," Reese said. "I don't belong with you guys." She began to walk away with the guards.

Baby Doll stepped forward. "No, you belong with us." She held out her hand to Reese, who was utterly starstruck. "We're cool with you being in the video."

"I . . . I . . . I . . . You . . . you . . . you . . . ," Reese stuttered.

"I think what she means to say is thanks," Bria piped up. "And she'd love to be in the video." She elbowed Reese. "Did I get that right?"

Reese was speechless but managed to nod.

"Then it's settled. Get this girl some Dolls' duds that fit," Rag Doll said. "I'm thinking silver sequins?"

"No!" Liberty howled. "It's not fair!"

"Haven't you learned anything?" Bria asked Liberty. "It's not fair that Reese has no home. It's not fair that there are hungry people on the streets. That's what's not fair. Not that you don't get to wear some glitzy costume!"

Bria stepped forward. "I think Reese should be the spotlight dancer. She can have my part."

"Oh, Bria!" her mother gasped.

"Are you sure?" her teammates said.

"I've never been more sure of anything, except maybe the diet of the earthworm," Bria answered.

"That's very generous of you," Jazzy Doll said. "I think this video could use two spotlight dancers. What do you say, Dolls?"

Candy Doll clapped her hands. "I say, *sweet!*"

Jane threw her hands in the air. "I give up! This video is getting more out of control by the minute!"

Bria spotted Miss Toni watching the action from a corner of the room with Reese's mom. Was she *actually* smiling?

Reese grabbed Bria and hugged her. "You are such an amazing friend," she said. "I can't believe I'm going to be in a Sugar Dolls video!"

"Better than that," Miss Toni said, walking over to them. "Reese, I was just talking to your mom and she said you danced and that you'd like to take a tap class at my studio after school?"

"I would!" Reese exclaimed. "But . . ."

"But what?" Rochelle teased. "You don't want to hang out with us now because you're a big music video star?"

"No!" Reese said. "It's not that at all." She looked at her mom. "It's just that we don't have money to pay for dance lessons."

"Who said anything about paying?" J. J. jumped in. "I'm teaching a new tap class every Tuesday, and I can use an assistant with a 'professional' music video résumé to stand in the front of the class. Whaddaya say, Reese?"

Reese nodded. "I say that would be awesome! You guys rock!"

"I second that," said Miss Toni. "Bria, great job."

"But we haven't even danced yet!" Liberty protested. "So how could she do a better job than me?"

"I wasn't talking about Bria's dancing," Toni replied. "I was talking about how she stood up for her friend. And that's what being a Diva is all about." She turned to Reese. "So you think you can cut it at Dance Divas?"

Reese glanced over at her mom. "Would it be okay?"

Her mom nodded. "It would be more than okay," she said. "Miss Toni has offered me some extra work at the studio. I'm going to help sew costumes, and before you know it, we'll have enough money to get our own place."

"I'm very happy for all of you," Jane said, pointing to her watch. "But time is ticking and I'm getting ticked off. You have three seconds to get in your spots! One, two . . ."

She didn't even have to finish before all the Divas, Dolls, and crew snapped to attention and took their positions.

Jane turned to Toni and J. J. and grinned. "And that, darlings, is how it's done."

CHAPTER 19

Five Minutes of Fame

It had been over three weeks since the Divas and Dolls shot the music video, and Bria had almost forgotten about it.

"Do you know what today is?" Reese said, finding her friend in the Divas' dressing room.

"Oh my gosh!" she exclaimed, checking her school planner. "Tomorrow is my next science quiz! How could I forget? I'm going to be up all night studying!"

"No! It's the world premiere of the Sugar Dolls' 'Heaven Sent' video! J. J.'s got the TV tuned to MTV in the tap studio so we don't miss it."

Bria looked up from her binder. "Seriously? Studying can wait!"

She raced into the studio where the rest of the Divas and Toni had already gathered. Gracie was passing around a bowl of popcorn.

"Did we miss it?" Bria asked breathlessly.

"Just in time," Scarlett said, handing her the popcorn. "We saved you a front-row seat."

The words WORLD PREMIERE VIDEO flashed across the screen.

"This is it! This is it!" Gracie clapped her hands. Scarlett shushed her.

There was a close-up on sunlight streaming through a stained-glass church window. Then a pair of blue eyes appeared.

"That's me! Those are my eyes!" Liberty squealed. "OMG! I'm in a video!"

"Great," Rochelle said. "Of course Mommy gave you a close-up."

The rest of the video featured the Sugar Dolls dancing and singing. The scenes changed between the interior of the church and the clouds.

"That is so cool." Gracie gasped. "How do they dance in the sky like that?"

"It's shot on a soundstage in front of a green screen," J. J. explained. "They're not really in the clouds, but it looks like it, doesn't it?"

Gracie nodded. "Yupsolutely!"

"It's very nice," Scarlett said, "but where are we?"

"There!" Gracie pointed at the screen.

Scarlett squinted her eyes, trying to make out seven tiny figures in the background.

"We look like ants!" Anya exclaimed. "Little sparkly ants."

There was another close-up—this time on Liberty's pouty pink lips.

"Oh, look! Me again!" She giggled. "My lip gloss looks so good."

"Scarlett, I think that's your foot," Bria said, pointing to a pair of white ballet shoes in the corner of the screen. "And I think that's my butt kind of fuzzy in the background."

Toni frowned. "I hope you get more on-screen time than that."

The camera zoomed in and the girls came into focus. "It's me! It's me!" Gracie cried, jumping up and down. Each girl got a brief close-up.

Then the camera panned in on Bria and Reese. They tapped down the rows of pews in the church, dressed in silver sequin tuxedos and top hats. The Dolls followed them down the aisles and out the church doors into the sunshine before floating off into the sky.

"That's us!" Reese screamed. "We look amazing!"

"Don't you think they look amazing, Liberty?" Rochelle elbowed her.

"I wouldn't go that far . . . ," Liberty grumped. "They look okay."

There was a final close-up of Liberty's hand waving good-bye.

"Look at my fabulous French manicure," she bragged.

"I think you were all fab," J. J. said. "You should be proud of yourselves."

"You think everyone in my school saw me

on TV?" Liberty wondered out loud. "They'll probably all want my autograph tomorrow morning."

"Maybe they'll make you an official Sugar Doll, Liberty. They can call you Stuck-Up Doll." Rochelle couldn't resist.

"And what would you be? Stupid Doll?" Liberty said, tossing an insult back.

"That's enough," Toni said, breaking up the fight. "I'd like to remind you all that you are Divas, not Dolls—and we have a new competition to start preparing for." She pointed her finger at the door. "I want everyone in that studio in three minutes . . . or else!"

"And I have a tap class to teach—you coming, Reese?" J. J. added, clicking off the TV.

"You bet! I'd rather be a Diva than a Doll any day," Reese said, hugging Bria. "You guys are the best."

Toni raised her hand. "I second that. Anyone else agree?"

Bria stood up and led the girls in the Divas'

cheer as they skipped out of the studio and back
to practice.

"I said we're Divas . . . Oh yeah!
We're fierce and we dance on air!
Did you hear me say it? Oh yeah!
Divas got moves! Divas got soul!
Everyone watch us rock and roll!"

Reese smiled. She felt right at home.

Glossary of Dance Terms

Arabesque: a move where the dancer stands on one leg with the other leg extended behind her at 90 degrees.

Attitude: a pose in which one leg is raised in back or in front with the knee bent.

Balancé: a rocking step shifting weight from one foot to the other by crossing the foot either in front or back.

Battement: a quick kick either high (grand battement) or low (petit battement).

Fondu: a lowering of the body made by bending the knee of the supporting leg.

Fouetté: a turning step where the leg whips out to the side.

Grand jeté: a large forward leap in the air that looks like a flying split.

Pas de bourrée: a move performed where the first leg pulls the other leg in tightly in small and quick steps.

Pirouette: a turn on one leg with the other leg behind.

Relevé: to rise up on pointe or on demi-pointe.

Sheryl Berk is a proud ballet mom and a *New York Times* bestselling author. She has collaborated with numerous celebrities on their memoirs, including Britney Spears, *Glee*'s Jenna Ushkowitz, and *Shake It Up*'s Zendaya. Her book with Bethany Hamilton, *Soul Surfer*, hit #1 on the *New York Times* bestseller list and became a major motion picture. She is also the author of The Cupcake Club book series with her eleven-year-old daughter, Carrie.